The Windsor Secret

Other books by Graham Fisher

Novels
The Raging Torrent
Villain Of The Piece
End Of The Line
Face Of Danger

As George Fisher
Operation V.I.P.
The Hostages

As George Heather
Green In Youth

Non-Fiction
In collaboration with Heather Fisher
The Queen's Travels
Monarch: The Life & Times Of Elizabeth II
Monarchy & The Royal Family
Charles & Diana: Their Married Life
The Queen's Family
Prince Andrew
Consort: The Life & Times Of Prince Philip
Charles: The Man & The Prince
Bertie And Alix
The Crown And The Ring
The Future King
Elizabeth: Queen & Mother

In collaboration with Ralphe M. White
The Royal Family

In collaboration with Michael McNair-Wilson
Blackshirt

The Windsor Secret

Graham Fisher

ROBERT HALE · LONDON

© Graham Fisher 1989
First published in Great Britain 1989

Robert Hale Limited
Clerkenwell House
Clerkenwell Green
London EC1R 0HT

British Library Cataloguing in Publication Data

Fisher, Graham, *1920—*
The Windsor secret.
I. Title
823'.914 [F]

ISBN 0-7090-3680-9

Photoset in North Wales by
Derek Doyle & Associates, Mold, Clwyd.
Printed in Great Britain by
St Edmundsbury Press Ltd, Bury St Edmunds, Suffolk.
Bound by WBC Bookbinders Limited.

Contents

For My Wife
(Who started it all when
she bought that 'fine old
Victorian davenport in
rosewood')

Author's Note

The memoirs of the Duchess of Windsor reveal that on Thursday, December 3, 1936 – only a week before the Abdication – she suddenly fled from Britain, slipping away under cover of darkness and boarding the Newhaven-Dieppe night ferry as 'Mrs Harris'.

The diaries of the late King George VI similarly reveal how he tried in vain all that weekend to see the brother he was destined to succeed, telephoning Fort Belvedere daily only to be 'put off'.

Why did Wallis Simpson, as she then was, flee Britain so precipitately when she had previously insisted on remaining?

Why was the then King Edward VIII so elusive that weekend?

Much of what I have written in explanation of these mysteries is documented fact or is based on fact. The remainder is necessarily speculation. Readers must decide for themselves where fact ends and fiction begins.

In reconstructing the events of 1936 I have endeavoured to make those persons actually involved as true to life as research permits. However, to bridge the gaps, I have been obliged to invent additional characters and any resemblance these may bear to actual persons, living or dead, is mere coincidence.

Prologue

I was just finishing the daily stint on my next book when I heard the swish of car tyres on the wet paving of the drive. A car door banged and a moment later there was the sound of a key in the lock as my wife let herself in. I finished the sentence I had been typing and went to meet her.

'You're late,' I said.

'I know. Jane wanted to go to an auction sale. We went in her car, so I couldn't leave till she did.'

'Hope you didn't buy anything,' I said, half jokingly.

She looked guilty and I knew that she had. 'Come and see,' she said. 'I'll need your help to carry it in.'

I followed her out to the car. She had folded down the rear seats of the hatchback to make room for her auction-sale acquisition.

'What in the world do we need with a davenport?' I asked.

'I thought it would look nice in that niche in the reception hall.'

'How much?'

'Help me to carry it in,' she said, evading the question.

Between us, we lifted it into the house and propelled it across the reception hall on its small brass castors and into the niche alongside the stairs. 'There,' said my wife, admiringly. 'It fits beautifully. I knew it would.'

'How much?' I asked again.

She opened her handbag and brought out a sale catalogue. 'That's it there – lot 106 – a fine old Victorian davenport in rosewood.'

She had written the sale price alongside in pencil. 'You

must be mad,' I said.

'Nonsense. It was a real bargain. A dealer offered me another hundred on top as I was leaving.'

'You should have taken it,' I said.

'I must get those rain spots off before they mark it.' She went off to fetch a duster. I slid out one of the drawers. Dovetailed. Certainly a well made piece. The sloping top lifted easily on its brass hinges. So did the small flat galleried section to the rear. Lifting it revealed a grooved pen-rest, a deep well to take writing paper, a shallower one presumably for envelopes, and two small shallow nests, one of which held a dusty inkpot.

'There's an inkpot missing,' I said.

'So?' she queried, setting to work with the duster.

She wiped the rain from the exterior of the piece, took out the drawers one by one and shook out the dust, dusted the inkpot and the pen-rest. The pen-rest moved fractionally from side to side as she dusted it.

'Sounds loose,' I said.

'I think it's meant to lift out.' She hooked a fingernail under one end and raised the pen-rest from the wooden brackets supporting it.

'What's that?' I asked.

The removal of the pen-rest had revealed another well similar to the one for holding notepaper. But wider. And this one had something in it.

'Probably some old writing paper,' said my wife.

Whatever it was, there was so much of it, jammed in so tightly, that it took several minutes of easing and fiddling to get it out. 'Let's hope you've bought yourself a load of old bearer bonds,' I joked.

No such luck, as it turned out. It was notepaper, some fifty sheets or so, good quality, yellowing with age, crammed on both sides with small tight hand-writing, the ink fading. I switched on the light and began to read. The very first sentence jolted me.

I have resolved to kill Mrs Simpson.

'What is it?' my wife asked.

'I'm not sure. Someone trying to write a novel, I think.'

There was no title; no author's name. I glanced at the last

sheet. No name there either.

'Don't keep it all to yourself,' my wife said. 'I was the one who bought the davenport – remember?'

'Let's sit down,' I suggested and led the way into the sitting-room. We sat side by side on the couch as I read through the manuscript, passing each sheet of notepaper in turn to my wife. It was well into the evening before we had both read to the end.

My wife sat there with the last sheet of the manuscript in her hand. 'I don't think it's a novel,' she said. 'It rings true. More like some sort of personal journal.'

'Then whoever wrote it really –'

'Yes,' she said, interrupting me. 'Wonder who it was.'

'Shouldn't be hard to find out.'

But there I was wrong. It was a task which was to take more than a year; take me to several different parts of Britain as well as to France and the United States. I started off by trying to trace the antecedents of the davenport. A telephone call to the auctioneer elicited the fact that it had been entered for the sale by a couple in Sevenoaks who had moved into a smaller property on the south coast. He gave me their new address and we drove there, my wife and I, the following weekend. A nice old couple but with fading memories of where and when they had acquired the davenport. They thought from an antique shop in Tonbridge a quarter of a century ago. Or was it Tunbridge Wells? Name of Sellars, they thought. Or was it Sales?

It was Sales, as I discovered after trips to both Tonbridge and Tunbridge Wells. But the Sales in question was long since dead and the antique shop was now a Chinese take-away. No hope of tracing the original ownership of the davenport.

That left the manuscript itself or 'the Journal' as my wife and I had come to think of it. Was it fact or fiction, an almost incredible segment of unknown recent history or the first draft of a good thriller? I obtained copies of the memoirs of the Duke and Duchess of Windsor[1] from our local library. Neither contained any direct reference to the curious sequence of events related by the unknown author, though parts of both supported what was written in the

Journal. A window of the Cumberland Terrace residence which the Duchess had occupied following her divorce from Ernest Simpson had been shattered. There had been a period of forty-eight hours over the weekend prior to the Abdication when the King (as the Duke of Windsor then was) had been, if not missing, certainly out of touch to such extent that even his brother, the Duke of York, had been unable to see or talk to him. I went through the Journal again, listing the names mentioned in it. Several I knew to be dead – the Windsors, Winston Churchill, the Lord Brownlow of that generation – but among the others there might be one still alive who would know the identity of the unknown writer.

First on my list was a journalist identified in the Journal only as 'Hugo'. Telephone calls to various newspaper contacts amplified the name into Hugo Morton-Hughes, long since retired but still alive, as far as was known. Last known address: a village north-west of Glasgow. I caught an early-morning flight to Scotland and did the rest of the journey in a self-drive hire car. Hugo was still alive, still at that address, but, sadly, now a senile old man unable to remember even the Duke of Windsor let alone a chance encounter in a club called 'Pink Flamingo' over half a century before.

My wife and I spent our summer holiday motoring over the same route Wallis Simpson had taken when she fled from Britain, Dieppe to Rouen, Rouen to Evreux, to Chartres, Orleans, Blois, Moulins, Lyon and eventually Cannes. It was in Evreux that we had our first stroke of luck.

He was an old man – *quatre-vingt-neuf*, he gave us to understand; short and squat; incredibly wizened. *Oui*, he had once been employed at the Hotellerie du Grand Cerf. *Oui,*he remembered *la Dame* stopping there. Would he ever forget it? That had been the day …

Had we been ordinary tourists we would have laughed off his story, regarding it as the sort of yarn a French *ancien*, indeed an old man in any country, will spin in the hope of earning himself a few francs or a free drink. But we were not ordinary tourists. We had read the Journal.

And his story, incredible as it might sound, was an echo of what we had read.

That was the extent of our luck in France. Still no clue to the identity of the author of the Journal. 'Give up,' my wife urged on our return home. 'You're never going to find out who wrote the wretched thing.'

'I have to,' I protested. 'Now more than ever. We know now that it's true.'

'You're letting it become an obsession with you,' she accused – and she was right.

I knew that I would never rest until I had found out the truth of what had happened during those few dramatic days preceding the 1936 Abdication and established the identity of the unknown writer who had been at the heart of it all.

I flew to New York where the files of the *Daily Record* produced the name of the journalist who had been Paris correspondent at the time of the Abdication. He too had long since retired and was living now in Alexandria, just south of Washington. Old as he was, his mind – unlike that of the unfortunate Hugo – was crystal-clear. He remembered much of what had happened in those days in the nineteen-thirties when he, in company with a score of other reporters and photographers, had pursued Wallis Simpson across France.

'Jeeze,' he said. 'There were a whole horde of us – American, British, French. I remember some of them, but durned if I remember anyone from the *Morning Post*.'

'Rode a motor-cycle,' I prompted him.

'You're right,' he said, and for a moment I thought I was going to find out what I wanted to know. Then he shook his head. 'Don't recall the name though. Don't think I ever knew it.'

I tried hard to refresh his memory, but it was no good. I returned to Britain no further forward. Then, a week or so later, I had a stroke of luck. I was leafing through the autumn edition of my publisher's catalogue when the name Curtis-Manners caught my eye. It was in the blurb for a new book by Anita Flitch: *It Girls of the Roaring Twenties*. 'Based,' it said, 'on the reminiscences of the author's grandmother, the Hon. Mrs Loretta Curtis-Manners.'

Curtis-Manners! The one name in the Journal which afforded a direct clue to the identity of the author ... *my aunt*. I had already spent hours in our local library, poring through the pages of *Who's Who* and *Debrett* in an endeavour to trace her, but without success.

I telephoned the publishing firm and spoke to the young lady who handled publicity. Somewhat reluctantly, even though I was one of their authors, she gave me Anita Flitch's telephone number. I called the number. A female voice answered.

'Miss Anita Flitch?' I queried.

'Miz,' the voice corrected me.

'Sorry,' I apologised. 'I was wondering, Miz Flitch, if you would tell me how I can get in touch with your grandmother, the Honourable Mrs Curtis-Manners.'

'You might try the cemetery at Nice,' she said. 'She died there about two years ago.'

'I'm sorry to hear that.' I said. 'I was hoping she could tell me where I might contact a nephew of hers.'

'Which one? Ours is a big family. What's this all about, anyway?'

I had nothing to lose by telling her the truth. Well, some of the truth. 'I've come across a manuscript which was apparently written by a nephew of hers. I'd like to return it.'

'You're sure it's a nephew?' she asked. 'Why not a niece?'

'I don't think so,' I said. 'Not from the context.'

'Spoken like a true MCP. Let me see now. Grandmother was one of nine children – no Pill in those days. They all married except for one, Great-aunt Polly. I don't know how many children they had between them – twenty-three, twenty-four, something like that. You'd do better to talk to Uncle Dukie. He's not really my uncle, of course. First cousin, once removed. I just call him uncle out of respect.'

I reached for my notebook and ballpoint. 'If you could give me his name – Mr – ?'

'You won't get far if you go calling him Mr. He's – ' She mentioned a title. Then she embarked on a display of feminism. 'If it wasn't for this primogeniture bilge, the title would have come to mother and then to me. She was the firstborn child of the firstborn child, but they both happened to be daughters and so didn't count.'

'You've been very helpful,' I said. With her uncle's title as a guide, I could look up the family in *Debrett*. And next day I did.

The family tree listed twenty-three names in the generation in which I was interested, twelve male and eleven female. Two were Anita Flitch's uncles, her mother's brothers. They would have written of Mrs Curtis-Manners as 'mother', not 'aunt'. I could discount them. Of the remaining ten, two had died in childhood and one would have been still at school in 1936 when the events in the Journal took place. I was down to seven. *Debrett* gave an address for the Duke and *Who's Who* added the addresses of three more, enough to be going on with.

I started with the second son of the youngest of the Duke's brothers, for no better reason than that he happened to be the most convenient, a partner in a firm of stockbrokers with an office not far from St Paul's. I made an appointment to see him, a tall man with a plummy voice and an arrogant manner. Two minutes' conversation was sufficient to make it clear that I had not found the author of the Journal.

I arrived home again to find a police car parked in the drive and my wife in a state of dither. 'We've had burglars,' she said. 'While I was out playing tennis.'

'What have they taken?'

'That's the funny thing. Nothing's missing.'

But the place had been thoroughly ransacked. Every drawer pulled out and emptied.

'Looks as if they were after something special,' said one of the policemen. 'You got a stamp collection, gold coins, anything like that?'

I shook my head. It wasn't until after the police had gone that it dawned on me that I did have something some people might class as 'special'. I went through to the lounge hall. Like every other drawer in the house, those of the davenport had been taken out and emptied. But the intruder had not found the recess hidden under the pen-rest. The Journal was still there.

The following day I did two things. I sealed the manuscript in a large envelope and took it round to the bank for safe keeping. Then I caught a train into London to have a chat with Miz Flitch.

She lived in a cobbled cul-de-sac in West Ken, one of those bijou town houses that cost the earth and afford the sort of accommodation a garden gnome would find scarcely adequate. Miz Flitch herself had cropped hair, was swathed in a kaftan and was smoking a small cigar.

I produced the list of names I had found on my visit to the library. 'The manuscript I telephoned about. I think one of these people may have written it. I'm hoping you can tell me where I might contact them.'

She studied the list. 'Uncle Dukie's easy. The ancestral home, Keston Castle. This one – George – is dead. Died earlier this year. William's in Guernsey. Tax exile. Harry's out of the country too. Been gone for years. Australia, I think. Or is it Canada? My mother would know.'

She had given me the opportunity I was seeking. 'Your mother doesn't know who might have written it, I suppose?'

'No. I asked her. Hasn't a clue.'

So she'd told her mother. Mother could have told some other member of the family.

Having found out what I really wanted to know, I made my excuses and left. But not before I had obtained her mother's telephone number and addresses for two other names on the list.

It was around five o'clock when I arrived home. My wife wasn't there, though that was hardly unusual. By six o'clock, when she still wasn't home, I felt the first little niggle of concern. I called our married daughter who lives about five miles away. No, she hadn't seen her.

I waited another half-hour before starting to call round our friends. She had had coffee with Jane in the morning but had left before lunch. None of them had seen her since.

By now it was a few minutes after seven and I was really worried, wondering what to do next. Call the local hospitals – there were three; call the police? The telephone rang. This had to be her. I whipped it to my ear.

It was a man's voice. Unnaturally deep and gruff. Disguised?

'Wondering what's happened to your wife?'

'What do you know about my wife?'

'Don't worry. She's safe and well. Want to do a swap? You've got something we want. Just divi up and your wife will be back in two shakes of a lamb's tail.'

'I can't imagine – ' I stopped short. Someone wanted the Journal. Badly. Yesterday's break-in hadn't found it. So they were trying another tack. 'What is it you want?' I asked.

'That writing you found – that book thing. There's a yellow bin at the end of your road. Holds stuff for gritting the road in winter. Do it up in a nice neat parcel and put it in there. In the next hour or I won't answer for your wife's safety.'

'I can't,' I protested. 'It's at the bank. I can't get it till tomorrow.'

'Tell that to the Marines. You've got one hour if you want wifey back safe and sound. Do it.' The line went dead.

I stood there, frozen, scarcely able to think. If it was a choice between my wife and the Journal, they were welcome to the damned thing. But there was no way I could get it until the next day. I had to do something. An idea came to me. It had to be one of the names on the list I had made. Not the stockbroker. Burglary and kidnapping were linked, and there had been no time for him to arrange the burglary. So it had to be someone Anita Flitch had told. Her mother? Or someone her mother had told.

I reached in my pocket for the list of names and dialled the number she had given me for her mother. A woman's voice answered.

'Mrs Flitch?' I asked.

'This is she.'

I gave her my name. 'I'm calling about a conversation I had with your daughter. About a manuscript I found.'

'Yes, she told me. But I don't think I can help you.'

'I think you can. Since I spoke to your daughter my house has been broken into and now my wife has been kidnapped. The kidnapper says he wants that manuscript.'

There was a moment's silence. Then she asked, 'Is this some sort of joke?'

'I wish it were, but I assure you it isn't.'

'Then you should call in the police. I don't know why you're calling me. I know nothing about it.'

'Well, someone does. Someone in your family. Someone you or your daughter told.'

She gave a small gasp. Then she said, 'No one in our family would do a thing like that.' But the gasp had given her away.

'Who did you tell?'

'No one. Well, only – no, I can't tell you. He wouldn't – '

'Listen to me, Mrs Flitch. It's me or the police. If I call the police, I shall certainly give them your name. And I'll make sure the newspapers know.'

There was another brief pause. Then she said, 'I did tell someone.'

'Who?' I demanded.

'I won't give you the name. But I'll ring him immediately and tell him what you've told me.'

'Tell him that if my wife isn't back within the hour, unharmed, I'll involve your whole family in the biggest scandal it's ever known.'

I replaced the telephone with a hand that was wet with sweat. I wiped my hand on my trousers; poured myself a drink. I paced restlessly around while the minutes ticked away with infuriating slowness. It was twenty-two minutes before the telephone rang again. I whipped it up.

It wasn't Mrs Flitch. It was a man's voice, quiet and cultured. 'Things would seem to have gone beyond what was intended.'

'Who is that?' I demanded.

'Don't worry – she's on her way home. I have already arranged that. I can only apologise. I never dreamed the people I employed would go to such lengths. Not kidnapping.'

'Burglary was all right, I suppose.'

'I'm sorry. I was concerned to protect the good name of the family. I'm afraid I didn't think beyond that.'

'Did you write the Journal?'

'The what? Oh, the manuscript you found. No, not me.'

'But you know who did?'

'Yes, I know that. I think we should meet. Tomorrow. Have lunch with me at my club.' He gave me the name.

Headlights flashed across the window as a car turned into the drive. 'I think that's my wife,' I said and banged down the telephone.

She was trembling as I helped her out of the car and into the house. 'It was terrible,' she said. 'I thought they were going to rape me.' She burst into tears.

I mixed her a stiff gin and tonic. Haltingly, disjointedly, between sobs, she told what had happened. Two men had moved in on her as she got out of her car at a supermarket carpark. She had been bundled into the back of the car, blindfolded and driven a few miles, then taken into some sort of building and told to sit on what felt like a couch. One of the men had gone off somewhere, leaving her, still blindfolded, alone with the other. He had been gone a long time. 'Bugger says he hasn't got it,' he announced when he finally returned.

'He would, wouldn't he?'

'I gave him an hour.'

The man had brought fish and chips back with him. They gave her some and a can of Coke to drink. Later, one of the men said, 'Well, I'm off to see if he's made the delivery.' But before he could leave there had been the sound of another car stopping outside and a third man arrived on the scene.

'I've just had the client on the blower. He's heard what's happened and doesn't like it. He says if we don't let her go he'll call the cops himself.'

So she had been bundled back into the car, driven away

and left. When she removed the blindfold she was back
where it had all started – on the supermarket car park.

I told her my side of the story, fed her a sleeping-pill and
helped her upstairs to bed. Next day, as arranged, I lunched
with the man with the cultured voice at his London club.

'I owe you an apology,' he said over the turtle soup.
'Perhaps this will serve to make amends. He slid a cheque
across the dining table. It was for ten thousand pounds. 'Of
course,' he added, 'I'd expect you to hand over the
manuscript.'

'No,' I said, and passed the cheque back.

'You can't use it. It's not your copyright.'

'Is it yours?' I asked.

'I didn't write it, if that's what you mean.'

'But you know who did.'

'Yes.'

'Then why not let him decide whether I can use it or not.'

He gave a curious smile. 'Waste of time,' he said. We
lapsed into silence as a waiter removed the soup bowls,
another served the fish and a third poured the wine. 'All
right,' he said when we were alone again. He brought out
an elegant fountain pen and wrote on the back of the menu.
'Try if you like.' He passed the menu across to me.

So I found myself finally at a hospice where the author of
the long-hidden Journal lay dying from cancer. I sat by the
bedside and explained the purpose of my visit. 'I'd like to
publish a book based on your Journal. This is a rough draft.'
I took the typescript from my briefcase and placed it on the
bedside cabinet. 'I hope you'll give permission. We'd share
the royalties, of course. I've drawn up a contract between
us.' I placed the contract on top of the typescript.

'I don't know. I'll have to think about it. Could you come
back in a month's time? I think I could read it by then.'

'Thank you,' I said and stood up. 'It's a remarkable story.
Is it true?'

The thin, ravaged face twisted into the semblance of a
smile. 'Tell you when you come back.'

But I was never to go back. The month was not quite up
when I received a telephone call from the matron of the
hospice. Death had intervened.

A few days later a package arrived in the post. In it was the typescript, a letter and the contract I had drawn up. To my amazement, the contract had been signed.

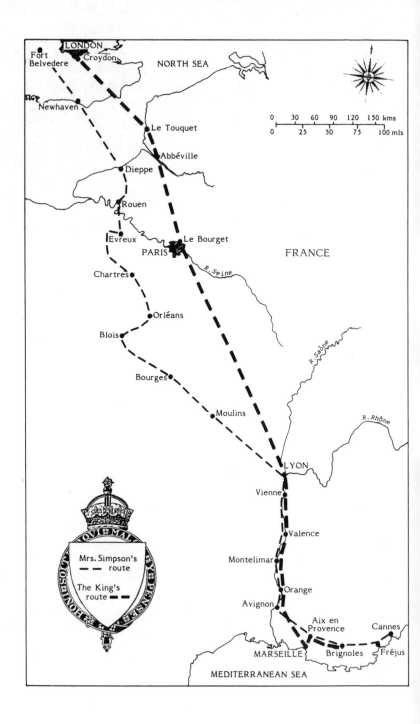

LONDON
Fort Belvedere
Croydon
NORTH SEA
Newhaven
Le Touquet
Abbéville
Dieppe
Rouen
Evreux
Le Bourget
PARIS
FRANCE
R. Seine
Chartres
Orléans
Blois
Bourges
Moulins
R. Saône
R. Rhône
LYON
Vienne
Valence
Montelimar
Orange
Avignon
Aix en Provence
Cannes
MARSEILLE
Brignoles
Fréjus
MEDITERRANEAN SEA

0 30 60 90 120 150 kms
0   25   50   75   100 mls

HONI SOIT QVI MAL Y PENSE

Mrs. Simpson's route
The King's route

1

Background
(October–November, 1936)

The hand-written Journal which came into our possession when my wife bought that 'fine old Victorian davenport in rosewood' was not really the beginning of the story. Its roots go back several years earlier still, perhaps to a day in the early nineteen-thirties when the future King Edward VIII, then still Prince of Wales, was a guest at a cocktail party given by Thelma[1] the American-born wife of Lord Furness. Among the other guests was an elegant and vivaciously dominant American woman in her mid-thirties. 'This is Wallis,' said Lady Furness, introducing her new friend to the Prince. 'She's just over from the States.'

But for the purpose of this book the story starts on an October day in 1936 when a man with the face of a worried bulldog emerged from 10 Downing Street and climbed into his car for the twenty-three-mile drive to Windsor. Stanley Baldwin, now in his third (though not successive) term as Prime Minister and his seventieth year, his health beginning to fail, had an audience with the King ahead of him and was not relishing the prospect. What he would be obliged to say would hardly endear him to the new monarch, less than nine months on the throne and not yet crowned.

Baldwin's request for an audience with the King had been precipitated by the news that Wallis Simpson had filed a petition for divorce. It was news which had travelled like a shock-wave through the upper ranks of British society, heard with horror by the new King's relatives – his mother, brothers and sister; by officials of the Royal Household; by the prime minister and members of his Cabinet. The case was set to be heard on October 27 in the quiet East Anglian backwater of Ipswich, birthplace of that Cardinal Wolsey who sat as a judge when Henry VIII sought to divorce Catherine of Aragon. If the judgement was in Mrs Simpson's favour she would emerge from court with a *decree nisi*. In another six months, on April 27, 1937, this would become a *decree absolute*, making her a free woman and with just sufficient time to marry the King before his coronation the following month.

Baldwin shuddered at the thought. That the King would seek to marry her once she was a free woman, he did not doubt. Worse, far worse, he would want her crowned beside him as Queen Consort ... a twice-divorced woman as Queen of England. Parliament would never stand for it; the nation would not stand for it. At all costs the King must be persuaded away from the dangerous course on which it seemed he was set to embark. Persuading him would not be easy, Baldwin knew. Perhaps impossible. The King was a self-willed man, spoiled by his long years as Prince of Wales, the blue-eyed darling of the British Empire; accustomed to his own way in everything.

Fort Belvedere came into sight with its mock towers and make-believe battlements. Situated on the edge of Windsor Great Park, it had been the new King's favourite retreat for several years past, a place where he could entertain his friends in privacy. Especially his lady friends, Freda Dudley Ward, Thelma Furness and others. And of late that special friend who had been Bessie-Wallis Warfield and had been twice married to become first Bessie-Wallis Spencer and now Wallis Simpson.

Alerted to the Prime Minister's arrival, the King came out to greet him, pipe in hand.

'Good morning, Prime Minister. Shall we take a turn round the gardens?'

'As Your Majesty wishes.'

They strolled in silence, neither wishing to be the first to broach the delicate subject both knew to be uppermost in their minds. The King was the first to speak. 'Say what you have come to say, Prime Minister.'

During the drive from London Baldwin had rehearsed half a dozen different ways in which he might approach the subject without causing offence. Danger lurked in all of them. There was, as he had come to realise, no completely safe way. So he began in roundabout fashion, asking the King if he remembered an occasion when the two of them had travelled together by train.

If the King was surprised by the question, he did not show it, but merely nodded, saying, 'That would have been – let me see – about eight years ago.'

Baldwin coughed diffidently. 'You said then, Sir, that I might speak freely to you about anything.'

'That is still so, Prime Minister,' the King said, encouragingly.

Baldwin braced himself for what he had to say next. 'Does it hold good, Sir, when there is a lady in the case?'

There was a long pause before the King finally said 'Yes' and the tone in which he said it was no longer encouraging.

But they had reached the heart of the matter and there could be no turning back. Nor, to do justice to Baldwin, had he any thought of turning back. He would say what he had come to say. He would phrase it as carefully and delicately as possible, but he would say it. Inevitably he would anger the King, but he would strive to be as conciliatory as possible. The King listened in silence, a nerve in his face twitching, as the Prime Minister urged that Mrs Simpson should withdraw her divorce petition, leave Britain and go abroad. 'You are her friend, Sir,' he concluded. 'She will listen to you.'

The King's pipe had gone out. Taking it from his mouth, he said, frostily, 'I have no right to interfere in the affairs of an individual, Prime Minister. It would be wrong of me to try to influence Mrs Simpson because she happens to be my friend.'

If the Prime Minister thought this so much humbug, he

was too experienced a politician to let his feelings show. Instead, he said, pleadingly, 'Must the case really go on, Sir?'

To that the King made no reply.

Increasingly desperate, the Prime Minister decided to take the bull by the horns. He would be failing in his duty, he said, if he did not point out the dangers of the situation. The matter was already the subject of tittle-tattle in the newspapers of other countries and those in Britain could hardly be expected to keep silent much longer. 'Sir,' he said, 'there is already gossip that you have in mind –'

He stopped abruptly, his flow of words halted by the look of fury on the King's face. Then a moment later, unable to contain himself, be burst out, 'Sir, I do not believe you can get away with it.'

The moment he had said it he knew he had gone too far and braced himself for the King's reaction. To his surprise, the look of anger faded from the King's face and he was amazed to hear the King say, 'For me, she is the only woman in the world, Prime Minister. I cannot live without her.' Though a man in his forties, he spoke like a love-sick schoolboy.

But at least the barriers were down and they were speaking man to man. Baldwin shook his head. 'I cannot believe you mean that, Sir. The people will not have it.'

Both knew, though it had not actually been put into words, that they were speaking now of marriage – a marriage which would see Mrs Simpson crowned as Queen.

The King stroked his lip with the stem of his pipe. 'I have mixed with my people, Prime Minister,' he said, slowly, thoughtfully, 'and I think I know them.' He did not actually say 'better than you do', but that was the implication behind his words.

Then he turned abruptly on his heel and began striding back the way they had come. Baldwin caught up with him. 'I know this, Sir, that the people expect a higher standard of their King.' Then silence fell again between them.

It was to be nearly a month before the two men, King

and Prime Minister, met again. By then Wallis Simpson's divorce petition had been heard and granted. Now it was the King who summoned the Prime Minister, and Baldwin had little doubt as to the reason for the royal summons.

It was damp and raw that November evening as he made the short journey from Downing Street to Buckingham Palace. The uniformed sentries slapped their rifle butts in salute as the car drove through the tall wrought-iron gates and into the palace forecourt. A liveried footman conducted Baldwin upstairs to a room where the King sat at a Chippendale desk which had been his father's before him.

'Good evening, Prime Minister,' the King said, standing up and waiting with barely concealed impatience for the double doors to close behind the footman. Then he came straight to the point.

'You and I both know why you are here, Prime Minister. So I will tell you at once that I intend to marry Mrs Simpson once her divorce has been made absolute.'[2]

It was no more than Baldwin had anticipated. Even so, he was surprised to hear the King state it so bluntly. He felt his years and failing health weighing heavily upon him. By contrast, the King looked like a man rejuvenated, his blue eyes bright and clear, his face relaxed, as though he had shed ten years since their meeting at the Fort a month before. Nor did he display any of the anger he had shown on that occasion as the Prime Minister launched into his carefully rehearsed argument. With him too there could now be no beating about the bush.

'Sir, before coming here I took the liberty of sounding out my colleagues and I must caution you that such a course of action would not meet with Cabinet approval.'

The King gave his quizzical smile. He had hardly expected that it would.

'The Government would resign, Sir. I would resign. The result would be a General Election in which Your Majesty's personal affairs would be the chief issue. I cannot believe you will wish to go along that path.'

'I mean to marry Mrs Simpson,' the King repeated obstinately. He came round from behind the desk and stood squarely in front of Baldwin. 'Even if it means abdication, Prime Minister.'

Baldwin, his arguments brought to nought, scarcely knew what to say. But he managed, 'Sir, this is most grievous news.'

The King was clearly determined to have his own way and it was a grim and obdurate Baldwin who left the palace that evening to return to the House of Commons. The King had thrown down the gauntlet – the threat of abdication – doubtless anticipating that the challenge would not be taken up. No doubt the lady had put him up to that, the Prime Minister thought. Well, they would both be proved wrong. The challenge would be taken up and he had no doubt of the eventual outcome, though the duel would not be an easy one and victory would leave a bitter taste in many mouths and might well cause irretrievable damage to Britain's ancient system of constitutional monarchy.

The Prime Minister gone, the King went along to his private apartment to take a bath and change his clothes for the evening, his mind relieved that at last things had been clearly stated. The threat of abdication was a formidable weapon. It would not come to that, of course. He would get his way in the end, as he always had.

He was to dine that night with his mother, Queen Mary, and his mood of elation was still with him when he arrived at Marlborough House, a short distance away. The brocade-upholstered lift took him up to Queen Mary's private apartment on the first floor. To his disappointment, as he walked into the sitting-room with its large portrait of his dead father and his mother's cluttered collection of bric-a-brac, he saw that she was not alone. As though sensing what lay ahead, she had ensured herself of reinforcements in the persons of his sister Mary, the Princess Royal, and one of his three sisters-in-law, his brother Harry's wife, Alice, Duchess of Gloucester. He did not mind saying what had to be said in front of Mary – he would have to tell her for himself sooner or later – but had no intention of letting Harry get the news second-hand through his wife.

His mother rose to greet him, curtseying stiffly before embracing him. He was now her King. Only after that was he her son. His sister and sister-in-law followed the old Queen's example and the four of them chatted of this and that until the steward announced that dinner was served. They ate in the dining-room with Queen Mary's collections of Chelsea and Ludwigsburg porcelain displayed around them. Dinner over, to the King's relief, his sister-in-law took her leave. 'I have something to say to you, Mama,' the King said as Queen Mary led the way to her boudoir.

She seated herself on the embroidered needlework of one of the painted satinwood chairs dotted about the room. The King remembered, as a small boy, watching her at work on that very embroidery. His sister took up a position slightly behind and slightly to the left of his mother's chair.

'Well, what is it you have to say, David?' his mother asked.

'Simply this, Mama. I intend to marry Mrs Simpson as soon as her divorce is made absolute.'

'Really, David,' said his mother, 'anyone would think we were living in Ruritania.'

'If I can't marry her as King and make her Queen, I shall abdicate.'

'Never have I heard such nonsense,' said Queen Mary briskly. 'You were born to be King, you are King and it is your duty to remain as King.'

'No, Mama. I cannot continue to reign as King without the woman I love beside me.'

'Don't talk to me of love. I did not marry your father for love. Duty is above what you call love.'

'I have the same right to happiness as any other man, Mama.'

'Happiness cannot be found at the expense of duty.'

'I have a duty to Wallis too, Mama.'

Queen Mary muttered something which ended 'that woman.'

Inwardly the King felt anger. Outwardly he contrived to remain calm and conciliatory.

'Wallis is a truly remarkable woman, Mama – clever, intellectual, perceptive.'

'Clever enough to have married and divorced two husbands, it seems.'

'She has been unfortunate in that respect. But she is a fine person, as you would discover for yourself, Mama, if only you would receive her.'

Queen Mary's answer to that was a curt and uncompromising, 'No – never.'

Behind his mother's back his sister gestured with her hand as though cautioning him not to pursue the matter. But the King was not to be deterred.

'But why not?' he persisted.

His mother looked him straight in the face. 'Because,' she said, 'she is nothing but an adventuress.'

It was the end of the conversation and the beginning of a rift which was to haunt the Royal Family through two generations.

The following day – November 17 – the King saw each of his brothers in turn and told them what he had already told Queen Mary and the Prime Minister. Their reactions were different, dictated by their differing personalities. The Duke of York, oldest of the three and next in line of succession, was horrified.

'Y-you can't abdicate, David,' he stammered. 'Y-you're the King.'

The second of the King's three brothers was more phlegmatic. 'I only hope it doesn't mean I have to leave the army,' grumbled Henry, Duke of Gloucester. 'I don't much care for princing it.'

Of the four royal brothers, the eldest and the youngest had always been closest, with the King helping George, Duke of Kent, out of more than one scrape in wilder, more youthful days. To him alone the King now confided the fact that his threat of abdication was really an attempt at constitutional blackmail. If things worked out as he planned, he told George, he had every hope that he would be able both to eat his cake and still have it ... marry Wallis Simpson and still occupy the throne.

'But if you marry Wallis, what will she be called?' George

asked.

'Why, Queen of England, of course.'

George could hardly believe his ears. 'You're really hoping to make her Queen?'

Of course. Why not, George?' The King grinned. 'Empress of India too.'[3]

2

The House Party
(November 20–23)

While the vast majority of the British people, thanks to the agreed silence of the newspapers, were still in the dark concerning the King's desire to marry Wallis Simpson, the facts were known to many in the upper ranks of society and beginning to spread beyond. The King had told his brothers. The brothers had told their wives and the Duke of Kent at least, as the published diaries of Sir Henry Channon would later reveal, had told others. The King's friends and advisers knew and some of them told their wives. Members of the Cabinet knew and some of them consulted others. Harmsworth, Max Beaverbrook and other newspaper proprietors had been long in the know. So had many editors and reporters, though nothing was printed. Servants at various big houses picked up scraps of gossip and passed them on to others. So the story spread by word of mouth until several thousand people knew of it in one form or another.

At a score of house parties, dinner parties, cocktail parties – that fad of the 1930s – it was the main topic of conversation that weekend, among them the house party at Keston Castle[1], the ancestral seat of the 12th Duke. Unlike Fort Belvedere, the Castle was a real one, its walls thicker than the length of two tall men lying end to end, its origins dating back to the days of William the Conqueror, though it had been much embellished and, to a degree, modernised over the years since. Family archives showed that Queen Elizabeth once slept there, as she slept in so many other ancestral homes during her regal progresses around her realm.

Since then, for nearly four centuries, the ducal family had been close to the throne. An early duke had lent money to Charles I in support of the royalist cause during the civil war; an early Duchess had been among the many mistresses of Charles II. The present Duke, in his younger days, had served briefly as an equerry to King George V and the King had stayed at the castle more than once during the pheasant season. So, on various occasions, had three of his four surviving sons, among them the new King in the days when he was still Prince of Wales. That had been some five years before and the Duke along with the Duchess, the grown-up son of his first marriage and the fourteen-year-old daughter of his second had stood on the steps of the castle to greet their royal visitor. 'The Duchess and I are old friends,' the Prince had said, smiling, when the Duke presented her.

On the Saturday evening, after dinner, the carpet in the drawing-room had been rolled back and there had been dancing to the music of gramophone records.

'You look as young as ever,' the Prince had murmured to his hostess as they circled the floor to the strains of Carroll Gibbons.

'Nonsense, David,' she retorted briskly though his whisper had clearly delighted her. 'Every woman changes in fifteen years.'

'Was it really that long ago?'

'Nineteen-sixteen, remember? At a party in Mayfair. There was a Zeppelin raid and you bundled me under a table. You said I'd be safe there.'

'And weren't you?' he asked, teasingly.

'From the Zeppelin, yes.' She was silent a moment. Then she said, 'I don't know what got into me over those next few weeks, a young married woman – '

He interrupted her. 'I missed you terribly when I was packed off to France.'

'And forgot all about me the moment you returned.'

'I didn't want to ruin your marriage. I heard you'd had a

baby.'

'Oh, yes.' She paused, then said, 'David, didn't you ever – '

But whatever it was she was about to say went unfinished as the gramophone record came to an end and the Prince escorted her back to her husband.

There was no prince among the guests for that later house party in November, 1936; only a member of the Royal Household and even he had been invited more for his handling of a gun than for any royal connection. The main object of the weekend was again the bagging of pheasants reared on the ducal acres and the Duke, regarded as among the ten best shots in the country, had elected to surround himself with guests of like ability. Saturday, from nine in the morning till dusk, had been spent downing pheasants, with the daughter of the Duke's second marriage, now a tomboyish nineteen-year-old who had shot her first pheasant at the age of ten and her first stag only three years later, making up a muster of eight guns.

The Duke had the best bag of the day, though his son, the marquess, had acquitted himself almost as well, as had a young baronet, though the baronet had slightly blotted his copybook by complaining that potting pheasants was 'unutterably boring' compared with bagging tiger in India. Others of the shooting-party had equally lived up to their reputations as marksmen with the solitary exception of a cabinet minister who, good shot though he normally was, had been unaccountably off form. He had much on his mind and found it difficult to concentrate, he said by way of apology.

By the standards of Keston Castle, the house party was not a large one. Fourteen of them, family and guests, gathered that evening in the dining-hall, a room of vast proportions rising two storeys to the massive beams of the vaulted ceiling. The Duke's famous collection of weaponry, pikes and muskets, swords and bayonets, adorned the stone walls of the dining-hall along with the mounted heads of creatures which had fallen victim to his marksmanship in Scotland, Germany, Africa, India and elsewhere. The long oak table was covered with a cloth of white damask upon which Georgian silver and crystal dating from Queen Victoria's day gleamed in the light of the huge chandeliers. Half a dozen liveried footmen came and went, waiting upon table under the eagle-eyed supervision of Sampson, who had been the Duke's batman in the Great War of 1914-18 and was now his butler.

The Duke sat at one end of the long table and the Duchess at the other. He was just turned sixty, red-faced and beetle-browed, a hearty, active man despite his years. She was over twenty years his junior, still beautiful in her late thirties, his second wife, the first having been killed in a car accident. The cabinet minister with much on his mind, a man with a fine war record, was seated on her right while on her left sat a younger man, a newspaper proprietor whose new-style Sunday newspaper was renowned for its lavish use of photographs and notorious for the titillating detail of its court reports. The Duke, more concerned to have stimulating company on either side than with the protocol of who sat where, had elected to sit between his daughter-in-law, the marchioness, a vivacious young chatterbox with cupid's-bow lips, and a slightly older but extremely elegant woman whose slim-fitting dress was designed to reveal the beauty of her long, supple backbone. She was, as everyone with the possible exception of the cabinet minister knew, the current mistress of the young baronet. The baronet himself sat beside the Duke's unmarried daughter, artfully placed there by the Duchess. He might have a reputation for wildness and a passion for fast cars, but time would presumably cure both and the elegant beauty was only his mistress, not his wife. The only other unmarried male present had been placed with equal skill on the daughter's right, though the Duchess did not have much hope in that direction. Nor, for that matter, would it really be a good enough match. He was a member of the Royal Household, a friend of the King, but with no money to speak of and set in his bachelor ways. The Duke's heir, to his dismay though he was too much of a gentleman to show it, found himself seated between the wives of the cabinet minister and the newspaper proprietor. He would much have preferred the company of the baronet's mistress and the young, pretty wife of a politician who had not yet aspired to cabinet rank but soon would if the eloquence of his conversation was anything to go by.

Because the subject of 'the King's companion' was hardly a suitable one for mixed company, though both sexes were dying to discuss it, conversation over dinner turned mainly on shooting, hunting, the Spanish civil war and the Italian conquest of Abyssinia. A fleeting reference to Mrs Simpson on the part of the politician's wife brought a quick frown of disapproval from her husband and an adroit change of subject on the part of the cabinet minister. But once dinner was over and the ladies withdrew, things were different. In both the dining-hall, where the men clustered around the Duke at one end of the table with cigars lighted and the port circulating, and in the pink drawing-room where the ladies sipped coffee and nibbled on chocolates, though both the Duke's daughter and the baronet's mistress opted for a cocktail and a cigarette, Mrs Simpson was immediately the main topic of conversation.

In the dining-hall Sampson the butler was now the only servant present, his position behind and slightly to the left of the Duke enabling him to hear clearly everything that was said.

The Duke drew on his cigar. 'There's a story going round,' he observed, 'that the King has threatened to abdicate. Surely not?'

All eyes turned towards the cabinet-minister. 'My lips are sealed,' he said.

'What about you, Harry?' the Duke's heir inquired of the member of the Royal Household. 'Surely you must know.'

'Not me, old boy. I know nothing.'

'I heard the same story,' said the newspaper proprietor. 'And from a pretty good source.'

'You mean the King actually intends to abdicate?' asked the lesser politician.

'I didn't say that. Threatening to do something and

actually doing it are two different things. I think he's simply trying to bluff Baldwin.'

The cabinet minister decided to unseal his lips. 'He won't get away with it,' he said. 'I know the P.M. He'll call any man's bluff – even the King's.'

'The King can't possibly abdicate,' said the Duke. 'It's unthinkable.'

'He'll have to if he wants to marry her. He's not only King – remember – but Defender of the Faith, meaning the Church of England. As such, he cannot possibly marry a divorced woman – twice divorced, in fact. The country would never stand for it.'

'The country as a whole knows precious little about it,' interjected the baronet. 'There's not been a word in the papers.'

'There will be if the situation isn't resolved quickly,' said the newspaper proprietor.

'If the situation isn't resolved quickly – and satisfactorily – heaven only knows what could happen.' This from the cabinet minister. 'It's a constitutional crisis of the first magnitude. The King must give her up. If he doesn't, then he'll have to abdicate. Either that or the Government will resign.'

In the pink drawing-room the ladies were more interested in Mrs Simpson herself than in the gravity of the situation.

'I was lunching at Claridge's on Thursday,' said the cabinet minister's wife, 'and guess who was at the next table but one.' All eyes turned in her direction. 'This Simpson woman all the talk's about.'

'What's she like?' asked the politician's wife. 'Is she devastingly beautiful?'

'Hardly. But there is something about her.'

'Must be to get her hooks into the King,' said the Duke's daughter.

'Let's talk about something else, shall we?' said the Duchess.

'Don't be so stuffy, Mummy. We're all dying to know what she's like.'

'I'll tell you what she's like,' said the baronet's mistress.

'When I last met her I thought – '

'You've met her?' asked the newspaper proprietor's wife.

'Yes. twice, in fact.'

The cabinet minister's wife, who had hoped her account of lunching at Claridge's would make her the centre of attention, looked slightly put out. The Duchess busied herself with coffee-cups. The others looked expectantly at the baronet's mistress.

'Do tell,' said the Duke's daughter-in-law.

'Well, let me see. She isn't beautiful. But she knows how to make the most of herself; how to dress. Elegant – I suppose that's the word.'

'Is the King really in love with her?' asked the politician's wife.

The baronet's mistress considered the question. 'He's certainly infatuated with her. It's a curious relationship. She treats the King like a little boy and he – '

'I don't think you should talk about the King like that,' interrupted the Duchess.

'Oh, but she does,' persisted the baronet's mistress. 'She has this curious trick of calling him Sir – '

'And so she should.'

'Yes, but not the way she does it. She puts an inflection into the word that turns it into a joke. Even curiouser, as Alice would say, the King seems to like it. The first time I met her was at Fort Belvedere. The King was laughing and talking with others and quite obviously she thought she wasn't getting enough attention. "Oh, Sir," she said. "I've broken a nail." The King went trotting off and came back with an emery board, hovering over her while she repaired the damage. You never saw such fuss. You'd think she'd broken a wrist at least.'

'Is she sleeping with him?' asked the daughter.

'Really, darling,' remonstrated the Duchess.

The politician's wife said, 'Perhaps she's withholding her favours in the hope that he'll marry her. Surely that's what a really clever woman would do.' Her eyes met those of the baronet's mistress and her hand flew to her mouth. 'I'm sorry. I didn't mean – I – ' Her words tailed off.

'Well, now,' said the baronet's mistress, in no way disconcerted, 'there could be more than one opinion as to that.'

'I think she's a tart,' said the daughter.

The others looked from the baronet's mistress to the daughter and back again.

'Darling, you really shouldn't say such things in polite company,' said the Duchess.

'I meant Mrs Simpson, mother.'

The politician's wife laughed, then stopped abruptly. 'Oh, that's all right then,' said the Duchess, weakly.

In the dining-hall too the men were skirting the question of whether the King and Mrs Simpson were sleeping together.

'I hear she's gone to Fort Belvedere again this weekend,' said the newspaper proprietor. 'Suitably chaperoned, of course. That aunt of hers.'

The lesser politician shook his head. 'Most unwise. She is not yet a free woman. The divorce isn't absolute. It could be quashed if she – ' He stopped, uncertain how to complete the sentence with delicacy.

'Beds with the King,' the younger baronet finished for him.

'But isn't that just what we want?' asked the Duke's heir. 'The divorce quashed? Then there can be no question of the King marrying her.' He grinned. 'Perhaps we should smuggle a private detective into Fort Belvedere.'

The Duke said, 'I hear the divorce case had something of a smell to it.'

The newspaper proprietor nodded. 'I don't think the judge was completely taken in.'

'But he granted it?'

'With reluctance – his very words.'

'You mean there was collusion?' asked the Duke's heir.

'Possibly.'

'If collusion could be proved, the King's Proctor could intervene,' said the Cabinet minister. 'Have the divorce set aside.'

'The King would never permit it,' said the member of the Royal Household.

'The King could hardly prevent it.'

'I think he could and he would. He's determined to marry the woman, come what may.'

'And you said you didn't know anything,' the Duke's son baited him.

Some thirty-five miles away as a crow flies, though half as far again given the winding nature of Britain's roads, the two persons under discussion were together in the library at Fort Belvedere. Wallis Simpson had been telling the King about that luncheon engagement at Claridge's witnessed by the cabinet minister's wife. Her companion at lunch had been Esmond Harmsworth, the newspaper proprietor[2]. From him had come a suggestion for a morganatic marriage, an expression she had not heard before. 'You would be the King's wife, but not Queen,' Harmsworth had explained.

The King shook his head as she recounted Harmsworth's idea. 'A morganatic marriage would be humiliating for you, Wallis.'

He no longer looked rejuvenated and invigorated, as he had done at his meeting with Baldwin, but tired and harassed. Subsequent meetings with two members of Baldwin's Cabinet on whom he had counted for support had not gone well. They might still speak on his behalf, he thought ruefully, but in the final analysis they would go along with their cabinet colleagues. There were few left he could really count on. Churchill. Beaverbrook. Not many more.

'I can stand a degree of humiliation if it keeps you on the Throne, David,' Wallis sought to reassure him.

'Well, I can't say I like it, but it may be the only way.' He stood up. 'I'll telephone Harmsworth immediately and get him to sound Baldwin out.'

At Keston Castle the gentlemen, lingering over their port, cigars and intriguing conversation, had not yet rejoined the ladies.

'What Mrs Simpson has given the King more than anything else is confidence in himself,' said the member of the Royal Household. 'He's always been very unsure of himself. Never really liked being Prince of Wales. If you ask me, Mrs Simpson is no more than a pretext for getting shot of a job he doesn't want. He'll cling to her for that reason, if for no other.'

'But he can't abdicate,' said the Duke. 'It's unthinkable.'

'Then there's only one thing for it,' said the young baronet. 'Eliminate his pretext.'

The others all looked at him. He grinned, sipped his port, elaborated. 'Have Mrs S come to a sticky end.'

In the pink drawing-room the ladies were debating what would happen if the King abdicated.

'He'll never abdicate,' said the Duchess, firmly. 'He's got too much sense of duty.'

'But suppose he did,' said her daughter. 'Would York become King?'

'He's got such a nice little wife,' said the politician's wife.

'Who – York?' queried the baronet's mistress. 'I think Kent would make a better King.'

'They say he's inclined to be a bit wild,' said the cabinet minister's wife.

'Princess Marina would certainly make a fine Queen,' said the wife of the newspaper proprietor. 'And they've already got a son to succeed him. The Duke of York has only two daughters.'

'And what's wrong with daughters?' demanded the unmarried daughter.

'Well, we certainly don't want Queen Wallis, do we?' It was more a statement of fact than a question from the marchioness.

'Certainly not,' said the cabinet minister's wife. 'Have you seen what the American papers are saying about her?' The others – all except the Duchess – craned forward eagerly. 'They say that after she left her first husband she lived by gambling. Playing poker. And she had an *affaire* wih some South American.'

'A woman like that should be shot,' said the politician's wife.

Conversation at this point was interrupted by the entry of the men. 'Who's for a game of bridge?' asked the Duke.

Eight of them made up two tables of bridge while the six

younger members of the house party danced to the music of gramophone records. All fourteen went to church the following morning and after lunch the cabinet minister and the newspaper proprietor, with their wives, climbed into their respective cars to return to London. Later that day the Duke's chauffeur drove the Member of Parliament and his wife to the station to board a train. The remainder of the house party stayed over Sunday night and the following morning, after breakfast, the young baronet and his mistress squeezed into a nifty sports car and roared off down the drive, scattering shingle in their wake. The member of the Royal Household donned a suit of leathers preparatory to setting off on his motor-cycle. The tomboyish daughter asked where he was going. 'London,' he said. She asked if he would give her a lift. 'On the pillion?' he queried, surprised. 'Why not?' she said. They went off together and soon after the Duke's heir and his wife set off, also by road, for their home in Buckinghamshire. The visitors gone, Sampson the butler sought out the Duke and requested a few days off. His father was seriously ill, he said. The request was readily granted, the more so as the Duke himself planned to spend a few days at his London residence which had its own staff.

The King and Mrs Simpson also travelled back to London that Monday morning in separate cars, the King heading for Buckingham Palace and Mrs Simpson making for her elegant Georgian house in Cumberland Terrace. She arrived there around the same time that Esmond Harmsworth was calling, by appointment, on the Prime Minister.

That the idea of a morganatic marriage did not find favour with the Prime Minister was quickly apparent. The constitution contained no provision for such a marriage, he told his visitor. Legislation would be required and he doubted that Parliament would pass it.

'But you will look into it,' Harmsworth urged.

The Prime Minister said he would. 'I will even place it before the Cabinet if that is what the King wishes,' he added, 'but I can do that, of course, only upon his personal request.'

His mission as the King's emissary concluded, Harmsworth left. Elsewhere in London, as he gave the King an account of his meeting with Baldwin, one of those who had been at Keston Castle over the weekend was embarking on a potentially much more perilous mission … but one which, if brought to a successful conclusion, would surely save the King from the consequences of his folly.

3

The Journal
(November 23)

Except for some degree of editing – mainly in the cause of punctuation – the manuscript is printed as written by the original author. G.F.

I have resolved to kill Mrs Simpson. It came to me in church on Sunday morning, with the sermon going on and on, that it is really the only solution. The King cannot conceivably marry a woman like that. Still less can she ever be Queen. But that, I believe, is what she is after. He won't abdicate. She will never permit him to abdicate. She will make him fight it out and God knows what the end will be. It could even mean some sort of civil war. He's terribly popular and rightly so. A lot of people would rally to his cause. In a sense, that's what I'm doing. With her gone, he will come to his senses.

I don't know yet how I am going to kill her. I don't fancy ending up in Pentonville Prison, where I believe those condemned to death spend their last few days. So I'll have to plan things carefully. A shot from a distance would seem the logical way. I'm a pretty good shot with a hunting rifle, though I say so myself. I bagged a buffalo in Kenya on the last safari, and a charging buffalo is not the easiest of targets. Of course I had a white hunter to help me track the buffalo in the first place. Now I've got to set about tracking down Mrs S. Find out her movements. J might know – he works at the Palace – but it would be dangerous to ask him. There's bound to be a big hue and cry when it's all over and he might remember me asking him. I've got to be careful. Cover my tracks from the start if I'm not to be caught.

*   *   *

I've found out where Mrs S lives. Well, near enough. It came to me all at once. If anyone would know it would be Hugo. Hugo writes a newspaper column. By Our Society Correspondent. *That's Hugo – the Society Correspondent. It's not terribly well written, but filled with interesting tittle-tattle. Hugo knows absolutely everybody who is anybody.*

I thought about going to his office to see him, but decided against it. It's the sort of thing he might remember later. In any case, I don't suppose he's in the office much except when he's actually writing that column of his. Most of the time he's out and about, talking to people, winkling out the latest gossip. I've run into him from time to time at most of the usual places, the cocktail bar at the Ritz, the grill-room at the Savoy, the Cafe de Paris, Mirabel's and other places of that sort. So I started making the rounds and finally bumped into him, accidentally on purpose, in the Pink Flamingo *a drinking establishment just off the King's Road which is the latest in-place.*

The Pink Flamingo *is supposed to be a club. You have to be a member before you can get in, though I never remember anyone checking very much. I am a member. At least I think I still am. In any event, the only person I saw as I walked in was the hat-check girl. Inside it was the same pink lighting you get there, day or night; the usual jazzy effect of glass and chromium. I spotted Hugo almost immediately. He was perched awkwardly on one of the bar stools, all arms and legs, rather like a larger-than-lifesize marionette, talking to Johnny the barman who has a reputation for mixing some of the best cocktails in London. Barmen like Johnny, I imagine, are useful sources of tittle-tattle for someone like Hugo.*

There were a few other people in the place, but no one I knew. Mainly couples, some of them fairies like Hugo, others probably men with other men's wives. Or women with other women's husbands. The Pink Flamingo *is that sort of place. I pretended not to have seen Hugo and sat down at a table, waiting until I could catch Johnny's eye. He came over.*

'What will it be?' he asked. 'A Pink Flamingo?'

The Pink Flamingo is Johnny's own invention, a mind-

boggling concoction of which Bacardi rum is the principal ingredient.

'I don't think so,' I said. I needed to keep a clear head. I ran my eye down the list of available cocktails: Maiden's Prayer, Manhattan, Bronx, Hong Kong Special, Charlie Lindbergh,, Jersey Lightning, Will Rogers, and decided upon a Gibson, which is a fairly straightforward combination of gin and dry vermouth.

Left alone at the bar, Hugo propelled himself around on his stool, recognised me and, as I had hoped, came over to my table, walking in that rather effeminate way he has.

'Hello, there,' he said. 'Long time no see. What brings you here?'

'Just killing time for half an hour,' I lied.

He sat down sideways at the table. Johnny brought me my Gibson, retreated again and Hugo asked, 'So what's the latest dirt?'

'I wouldn't know,' I said. 'And I wouldn't tell you if I did.'

'That's not nice.'

'Sorry,' I apologised. I didn't want him walking off until I'd found out what I wanted to know. 'That was rude of me.'

'Not to worry. All is forgiven. Anything new going on?'

'Not a lot. All anyone seems to talk about these days is that Mrs Simpson.'

'I know,' Hugo sighed, languidly. 'And I can't print a word. Such a bore.'

'I'd have thought it was just your sort of stuff, Hugo,' I said. 'So why don't you write about her?'

'Orders from up top. From God's-in-his-heaven-all's-right-with-the-world. Not a word to be published. But it can't last much longer. Some paper is going to break the truce and then you'll never stop reading about it.'

'Is she really the King's mistress?'

'That would be telling,' he said, coyly.

I sipped the Gibson. 'If she's living with him at the Fort, she must be.'

'Who says she's living at the Fort?'

'Well, the Palace then – no difference.'

I hoped Hugo couldn't resist showing how knowledgeable he was. He couldn't. 'Not the Palace either,' he said, 'though I've reason to believe she does spend her weekends at the Fort. But she

lives up by Regent's Park – in Cumberland Terrace.'
I didn't dare ask him whereabouts in Cumberland Terrace. I didn't want him remembering our conversation later.
'They were saying the other night that the King may abdicate,' I said.
'Who was?'
I shook my head. 'I'm not sure exactly who said it. It was at a dinner party.'
'Doesn't matter,' he said. 'I couldn't write it even if it was the P.M. himself.'
'Oh, it wasn't him,' I assured him smiling.
'Who was at the dinner party?' he asked. I knew he was fishing for something for his column. He deserved a small reward. So I told him what names I could remember. 'Boffy,' he repeated when I mentioned one particular name. 'That's interesting.'
'Why?' I asked.
'Ah,' he answered cryptically.
Now that I had found out what I wished to know, I wanted to get away. I had things to do. But I had to keep it casual. So we continued to chat of this and that, with Hugo dissecting people with that acid tongue of his. Then Denny Porter drifted in and came over to our table. 'Hugo, dear boy. Just the chappie I wanted to see.' He sat down and asked what we were drinking. I looked at my watch.
'Not me, thanks. I have to dash.' I finished my Gibson and made my escape.

*   *   *   **

At that stage I didn't really have a plan. I knew that I was going to shoot Mrs S, but the when, where and how of it did not yet exist. First I had to find out exactly where she lived in Cumberland Terrace, whether she was actually there, how and when she came and went. But even before that I had to find a suitable pied-à-terre to serve as a base camp. And I had some shopping to do.
Tracking down Hugo had necessitated going without lunch and I was going to have to eat if I was to function efficiently. I could both eat and shop in the West End.
I was about to hail a taxi when a thought struck me. I had used taxis for tracking down Hugo, but it wasn't wise to go on using

them. Taxi journeys could be traced and I didn't want Scotland Yard putting my movements together later.

I waited at a bus stop and boarded a bus instead. It was the first time I had been on a bus in years, trains yes, but not buses, and I found it an odd experience. I got off at Leicester Square and set about shopping. I walked up Charing Cross Road until I came to an army surplus stores. At least that was how it described itself, though there were a lot of items displayed in the windows that certainly weren't army surplus. I went in and bought myself a coat. It was on the large side and far too long. But that was how I wanted it. In one of the narrow streets linking Charing Cross Road with Shaftesbury Avenue I found the premises of a theatrical costumier. From him I bought a wig, a red one, saying I wanted it for amateur theatricals. I located a Woolworth's and made my way to the spectacle counter where I tried on several pairs, settling finally upon a pair of hornrims with lenses that were little more than plain glass. My final call was on W. H. Smith where I bought a street map of London. For all my purchases I paid cash.

Carrying the packages containing my various purchases, I went into the Lyons Corner House in Coventry Street. They had finished serving lunch, but had a range of cooked snacks available. I ordered Welsh rarebit and a pot of tea. I studied the street map while I was waiting to be served and located Cumberland Terrace.

The meal over, I made my way down the marble steps which led to the toilets in the basement. I slid a penny into the slot and bolted myself in. I put on the coat bought in the Charing Cross Road, the wig and the spectacles. Long and shapeless as it was, the coat – over the top of what I was already wearing – would serve to give a very different impression of my height, build and social status. I checked my new look in a mirror above one of the wash-basins. The wig was a bit skew-whiff and I adjusted it before walking back up the marble steps, threading my way between the tea-tables and going out into the street.

A bus took me to Marylebone Road and I walked through Park Square to the Outer Circle of Regent's Park. It was still only mid-afternoon, but the November daylight was already fading. I had memorised the route I must take from the street map and had no difficulty in finding my way to Cumberland Terrace, though the walk was longer than I had anticipated. Running parallel *with the Outer Circle and separated from it by its own narrow strip of garden, Cumberland Terrace is surely the grandest of the terraced Georgian residences John Nash designed to overlook the new park he landscaped for the Prince Regent on the site of the old Marylebone Gardens. Now one of those residences was the pied-à-terre of the lady known as 'the King's companion'. But which one?*

I walked the length of the terrace, not loitering, but not hurrying either. A yellow mist was beginning to creep over the area, generated as it always is at this time of year by London's countless coal fires. On the other side of the road, as I emerged again into the Outer Circle, I spotted a substantial building standing some 50-100 yards inside the Park. I crossed over to read the board fixed to the wrought-iron gates: St. Katherine's. It looked like either a hospital or a hospice. Either way, the building itself and the grounds in which it stood might well repay inspection in broad daylight.

It was almost dark now; raw and damp with it; the fog thickening, though it was not yet so murky as to render the street lamps completely ineffective. Now that I knew the whereabouts of Mrs S, I needed a base camp from which to operate. Nearby but not too near. I set out to explore the criss-cross of narrow, meaner streets to the east. They too were streets of terraced dwellings, but this was the only fact they had in common with Cumberland Terrace. The residences there were large, Georgian and gracious. Now the houses on either side were small, Victorian and ugly with their walls of blackened brick and lack-lustre paintwork. It had been a long day and I had almost decided to postpone my search for a base camp until tomorrow when a convenient street lamp illuminated what I was seeking. It was a card in a window: Room To Let.

The door had a rusty iron knocker shaped like a lion's head and stiff to the touch. I knocked twice with no response. A third knock produced the scuff of footsteps inside and the door was opened by a thin, angular woman in a long shapeless dress. 'Yes, wot is it?' she asked.

'I've come about the room,' I explained.

'I don't do no meals,' she retorted, ambiguously.

'That's all right.'

'So long as you understand.' She studied me suspiciously for a

moment, then said, 'You'd better come in.'

She drew back and I found myself in a narrow, low-ceilinged hallway with a mildewed print of Monarch of the Glen – or was it The Stag at Bay? – on one wall and a hallstand against the other. An unshaded bulb gave a feeble yellow light. To my dismay, a policeman's helmet hung on the hallstand. The woman saw me looking at it. 'I keep it there to scare away varmints,' she explained to my relief. 'Well, close the door,' she went on. 'Keep the cold out. This way. Follow me.'

I followed her along the hall and up a flight of creaking stairs covered with well-worn linoleum. Another unshaded bulb illuminated a narrow landing running front and back. The landing was papered in fading pink roses. Beyond a small archway we went down two steps. 'Bathroom,' said the woman, indicating a brown varnished door on the left. Up two steps brought us back to the original level of the landing and to another brown varnished door. 'This is it,' she said, opening the door and switching on a light.

It was a small room and looked smaller than it was because of the low, sloping ceiling. The wallpaper had an indeterminate trellis pattern with a patch of damp in one corner. There was a small window though it was too dark to see what it looked out on. A single bed with brass knobs top and bottom was crammed into the far corner. In another corner was an angled wash-stand with a jug and basin on it. There was a chair with a cane seat beside the bed and under the window was a small table covered with oil-cloth on which stood an ancient gas-ring. Beside the window was a wooden shelf on which stood a kettle, a small blackened saucepan and one or two other oddments.

'Rent's a pound a week,' said the woman. 'Baths is extra. Tanner a time. Gas works off a meter. Shilling in the slot.'

'It will do nicely,' I said. 'I'll move in tomorrow if that's all right.'

'I'll want a week's rent in advance.'

She held out a bony hand and I gave her a pound note.

'No cooking,' she said. 'Don't mind you heating up baked beans or suchlike for breakfast or making a cuppa cocoa at night. But no stews or nothin'. Stinks the place out. Up to you to keep your room clean.' That suited me fine. I didn't want her nosing around. 'Don't mind doing a bit of washing for you,' she went on.

'Tanner a time. I wash Mondays.'

'I'll remember that,' I said. With any luck, I wouldn't be there the following Monday.

'I don't know your name.'

I said the first name that popped into my head. 'Davis.'

'I'm Mrs Martin. You work round here?'

'Near Regent's Park,' I lied. Like most people who are not used to lying, I proceeded to elaborate. 'At St Katherine's.'

'I got this bad hip,' she said. 'Perhaps you could tell me what I ought to do about it.'

I shook my head. 'I don't know anything about hips, I'm afraid. I'm on the administrative side.' Inevitably, one lie was leading to another.

She sniffed. 'Paperwork, you mean.'

She led the way out of the room, along the landing and down the stairs. 'There's just one thing,' I said. 'I don't know if it makes any difference. Often I have to work late at night.'

'I'll give you a key. Tomorrow. Just don't make a noise if you come in late.'

'Oh, I won't,' I promised.

'You going back to work now?' she asked.

'No,' I said. 'I've only just started there. I have to get my things from the other side of London. Where's the nearest place I can get a taxi-cab?'

The moment I had said it I knew it was a mistake. 'They must pay you well at that hors-spittle,' she said. 'You won't get no cab around here. There's a Tube station in Euston Road. Don't want to go wasting your money on cabs.' She opened the front door. I took a quick look at the number above the lion's head knocker. 'That way,' she said, pointing. 'Turn right at the end. Then keep walking till you come to Gower Street. That'll take you to the station.'

'Thanks,' I said. 'See you tomorrow then.'

She closed the door on me. I paused at the end of the street to look at the name-plate. Toddington Crescent. It was a long walk to Euston Road station. Once there, I went into the public lavatories, removed the wig and spectacles, tucked them into the pockets of the second-hand coat, took off the coat and carried it over my arm. Then I went out of the station again and hailed a cruising cab.

4

The Journal
(November 24)

'What in the world's that?' Mrs Martin asked when I arrived at Toddington Crescent the following morning. She was wearing the same long, shapeless dress as the night before, with a stained apron tied round her waist.

'Golf clubs,' I said, dumping my suitcase in the narrow hallway, but keeping the golf-bag slung over my shoulder, the woolly coverings of the Nos. 1 and 3 woods serving to screen the tip of the Mannlicher-Schoenauer hunting-rifle hidden among the golf clubs.

Her eyes narrowed. 'I thought only rich folk played golf.'

Rich? Well, I suppose I was. Certainly by her standards. 'Not necessarily,' I said.

'You know the way up,' she said and stood there, wiping her hands on her apron and watching me as I picked up the suitcase again and trudged up the stairs. I went into the small, dreary back room which was to be my home for the next few days and closed the door behind me. I set down the suitcase and dumped the golf-bag on the bed. My arms and shoulders ached from the effort of carrying them all the way from the station – I had deemed it unwise to arrive by taxicab – and the red wig, which I had put on, together with the spectacles, in the station lavatory, a foul-smelling place, had given me the beginnings of a headache. I took it off and felt better.

I looked round for somewhere to conceal the Mannlicher. There was no reason why Mrs Martin should be suspicious, but she was certainly inquisitive and her inquisitive nature might find her *taking a look at the golf clubs in my absence. If she did, she was bound to see the rifle. The room afforded few opportunities to conceal anything larger than a sixpence. Then I had an idea. I propped the golf-bag in a corner, rolled back the mattress and bed linen, which was hardly as white as I was accustomed to, and hid the Mannlicher between the mattress and bed springs. I replaced the mattress and bedlinen and lifted the suitcase on to the bed. I had stocked up from the larder as for a hunting-expedition – tea, cocoa, sugar, condensed milk, biscuits, chocolate, some potted meat, tins of baked beans, sardines and corned beef. The multiple gadgets on my Swiss hunting-knife included a tin opener. I had also brought along a hip-flask of brandy, Courvoisier. I put the foodstuffs on the little table alongside the gas ring. I had kept clothes to a minimum – a change of underclothes, a pair of stout walking-shoes, a warm tweed jacket and a pair of plus-twos used previously for stalking in Scotland. I left the clothes in the case, closed it and locked it, and was in the act of sliding it under the bed when I heard footsteps coming along the landing.*

The wig! I remembered it in the nick of time. It was lying on the bed. I straightened up, reached for it and pulled it on. Wrong way round. There was a tap at the door.

'Just a minute,' I said.

I looked round for a mirror. There wasn't one. A glass-covered sampler on the wall afforded sufficient reflection for adjustment. I opened the door.

'I brought you a key for the front door,' said Mrs Martin. 'Mind you don't lose it. And make sure to give it back when you leave.'

'Of course,' I said. 'I wonder if it's possible for me to have a key to this room as well.'

'It don't have no lock,' said Mrs Martin. 'Don't need one. There's only me and you in the house.' She sniffed. 'I'm an honest woman.'

'Oh, absolutely,' I said. 'It was privacy I was thinking of.'

'I shan't disturb you more'n's necessary.' She sniffed again and shuffled out.

I sat on the bed, opened the map of London and worked out the best route to Cumberland Terrace. I re-folded the map, put it away, went downstairs, walked along the narrow hallway towards the back of the house and tapped on the kitchen door. It opened on a cloying smell which was a mixture of cooking, drying clothes, stale air and body odour.

'You again,' sniffed Mrs Martin. 'What is it now?' Clearly she had not yet forgiven me for wanting to lock my room.

'I'm just off to the hospital,' I lied. 'Don't quite know when I'll be back.'

'Suit yourself. You've got a key,' she said, and closed the door on me.

A man with a dirty sack draped over his shoulders and his cap on back to front was humping a bag of coal into the next-door house from a horse-drawn cart as I let myself out into the street. It was a typical November morning, grey and damp. I had worked out a short cut to Cumberland Terrace. Walking, I debated the tricky problem of finding out which was Mrs Simpson's house. I could ask a postman if I saw one, but that could be dangerous. Later, when the inevitable hue and cry developed, he might remember being asked ... even if it was by someone with red hair and wearing glasses.

Luck was with me, however, and I arrived at Cumberland Terrace to find a large car, a Buick, parked outside one of the residences and a small group of inquisitive onlookers huddled nearby. There were a couple of women of the working class with shopping bags, a small girl, an errand boy with a bicycle and an elderly man with a dog and a walking-stick. The front door of the residence was open and a uniformed chauffeur stood at the top of the steps. Beyond him, in the shadow of the doorway, was a woman.

'That her?' I heard one of the women ask.

'Dunno,' her companion replied. 'Never seen her, have I?'

' 'Taint her,' the errand boy chipped in. 'I see her come out the other day.'

'How do you know it was her?' the man asked.

'Wearing furs, weren't she? Had to be, din't it?'

'You talking about Mrs Simpson?' I asked, mumbling the words in an attempt to conceal my upper-class accent.

'We was wonderin' if that was her,' said one of the women. 'Do you know?'

'No,' I lied. In fact I had seen her on two occasions, though only once close up. 'Is this where she lives?'

'Is now,' said the woman. 'Since she got her divorce. Reckon *that's her car. Posh, aint it?'*

'*Hope she's going out,*' said her companion. '*I want to see what she looks like.*'

They were to be disappointed. The door closed, the chauffeur came down the steps, climbed into the Buick and drove off. I could now see the number on the door – 16. I knew my quarry's lair.

The elderly man limped away on his stick and the errand boy pedalled off on his bicycle. The two women stood gossiping a moment or two longer while the small girl wiped her nose on her sleeve. I stayed with them, silently counting the street lamps along Cumberland Terrace as a way of locating the correct residence after dark. It would have to be a snap shot. The target would be in my sights for only a few seconds, while descending or mounting the steps. On the flat there would almost certainly be the Buick obscuring the line of fire. I needed an elevated firing-point.

The strip of garden fronting Cumberland Terrace contained only shrubs and a few leafless trees, far too small either to support me or to afford adequate cover. I left the two women to their gossip and set off to explore further. There were more trees on the far side of the Outer Circle, in the grounds of the hospital, hospice or whatever it was, but they too were slender and leafless. I crossed over, went through the wrought-iron gates and followed a small path which led off the main drive. If anyone challenged me, which was unlikely, I would say that I was on my way through to the main part of Regent's Park. Walking slowly, I saw that one part of the building was clad in scaffolding. A couple of workmen were perched on the scaffolding, re-pointing the brickwork. The scaffolding was on two levels, along part of the front and down the side. Towards the rear of the building a ladder was set against the scaffolding and it seemed to me, though it was impossible to be sure at a distance, that it was lashed in place. If so, then it would probably stay where it was when the workmen were through for the day.

At the rear of the building a small gate gave access to Regent's Park. I went through it and found myself not far from the bandstand. I returned to the grounds, continued round to the front of the building and then out the way I had come, counting the number of paces it took to reach the main gate. I continued counting as I crossed the road in the direction of No.16. A

comparison with the Outer Circle enabled me to estimate the
width of Cumberland Terrace and the strip of garden fronting it.

I made my way through to Albany Street where I lunched off
cheese sandwiches and a glass of port in the saloon bar of a public
house. Between bites and sips I converted paces into yards on the
back of an old envelope and calculated the range. One hundred
and fifty yards, give or take a few yards either way. I had brought
down more than one stag over a greater distance. That had been
in daylight, but there was a street lamp almost outside No.16 to
afford sufficient illumination of the target at night.

There remained the question of getting away quickly and safely
once the job was done. Designed as it was to be slung over one
shoulder, the golf-bag in which I proposed to transport the
Mannlicher would impede my descent from the scaffolding. An
idea came to me and I inquired of the potman if there was a
harness-maker in the vicinity. There was one in Camden High
Street, he told me, and I made my way there from the public
house. The harness-maker was an old man, round-shouldered and
grey-haired, with a scarred leather apron fastened round his
waist. I told him I wanted a strap long enough for fastening
round a trunk. He went into a back room and came back with a
strip of leather. 'That do?' I nodded and watched while he
punched a series of holes in one end and riveted a buckle to the
other.

Leaving with my purchase, I spotted a cycle repair shop next
door. There was a new bicycle in the window of the shop and some
half-dozen second-hand ones in a rack on the pavement. A bicycle
would speed my getaway. The owner of the shop emerged as I
inspected the second-hand models, a small man with a balding
head and shifty eyes.

'How much is this one?' I asked.

'To you – five bob.'

I paid him and wheeled the bicycle away, not daring to mount
it until I was in one of the quieter streets. It was ages since I had
last ridden one, but they say once learned, never forgotten. There
were a few initial wobbles and then I had the hang of it again.
With my sense of direction, I had little difficulty in finding my
way back to Toddington Crescent. Some boys were playing
football in the street, their ball consisting of a bundle of rags tied
with string, their goalposts a couple of chalk marks on the

brickwork of a house. I held on to the bicycle with one hand while I fumbled for my key and unlocked the door with the other.

'Mrs Martin,' I called.

She came shuffling through from the kitchen at the back. 'Oh, it's you,' she said.

'I wonder if I could leave my bicycle in the hall,' I asked her. 'It might get stolen if I leave it outside.'

'You didn't say nothing about no bike.' Three negatives this time. I wondered what was the most she could string together.

'I've only just bought it,' I explained.

'Suppose you'd better bring it in then,' she said, grudgingly.

I wheeled the bicycle inside, propping it against the wall and closing the door behind me. 'I'm very grateful,' I said.

'It'll cost you another tanner a week,' she told me.

I went upstairs to my room, closed the door and took off the coat, glasses and that wretched wig. It had again given me the beginnings of a headache. I emptied out the golf-bag and, against the possibility that Mrs Martin might decide to look in on me, carried the bedside chair across the room and sat with my back against the door. Using my hunting-knife, I cut a slit in the bottom of the golf-bag, uncoiled the leather strap I had bought and threaded it through, catching hold of it again where it emerged at the top of the bag. Standing, I positioned the bag diagonally across my back and fastened the strap bandolier-fashion at the front. Now I had both hands free for whatever climbing I had to do. What was needed was a dummy run to assess the risks and opportunities. In case the risks outweighed the opportunities, I decided against taking the Mannlicher. But I needed something in the golf-bag to simulate its size and weight. I sorted out a selection of golf clubs which came to approximately the same weight and tied them firmly together, top and bottom, with a couple of handkerchiefs. Then I slid them into the golf-bag upside down, club heads at the bottom where the main weight of the Mannlicher would be on another occasion. My preparations complete, it was now simply a question of waiting until after dark.

Dark? The law required bicycles to carry lights during the hours of darkness and my newly acquired machine didn't have any. Still time to get to the cycle shop again before lighting-up time. I put on the coat, wig and glasses again and went *downstairs, walked along the hall to the kitchen and tapped on the door. Mrs Martin answered without opening it.*

'Yes, what is it?'

'I'm just going out again, Mrs Martin. Shan't be long.'

'I gave you a key, din't I? You don't have to tell me every time.'

I manoeuvred the bicycle out through the front door and cycled back to the shop, where I equipped myself with a front lamp and a red tail lamp. Purchasing them revealed another potential flaw in my planning. Funds were running low and there was no telling when I might need money in a hurry. I had an account with Coutts in the Strand. It was too late to go there that day, but I resolved to draw out £50 the following morning.

Back to Toddington Crescent, lights on fore and aft though it was not yet fully dark. Upstairs again, I checked my watch. Must remember to keep it wound. Time, like money, might yet prove to be a critical factor. Mrs S, if she was going out that evening, would probably leave No.16 somewhere between seven o'clock and eight thirty; would return, I imagined, between half past ten and midnight. I felt a sense of excitement stir inside me. I brewed myself some tea on the rusty gas ring and nibbled some biscuits. The condensed milk made the tea taste over-sweet and sickly. Then I lay on the bed to rest. The mattress felt lumpy, which was perhaps as well. I mustn't risk falling asleep. What I needed was an alarm clock. I got off the bed again, found my diary and made a note: 1. Money. 2. Alarm clock. The dummy run would probably reveal other items.

I lay down on the bed again, eyes closed but brain wide awake, my thoughts running ahead of me. I thought of Mrs S only as a target, a stag with malformed antlers which had to be cropped for the good of the herd. To think of her as a human being, a woman, might cause my resolve to weaken. She was a predator to be tracked down and eliminated in order that the King might survive. He would grieve, I imagine, but that would pass.

* * *

At six o'clock I began my final preparations. I changed into the plus-twos and tweed jacket. Then the long overcoat I had bought, the wig and the glasses.

If possible I had to leave the house without Mrs Martin seeing me. Inquisitive as she was, if she saw me she would surely wonder what I was doing with a golf-bag over my shoulder at that time of night. Leaving the golf-bag behind me for the moment, I went downstairs to spy out the land. There was the sound of voices from behind the door into the kitchen and I thought at first that Mrs Martin must have a visitor. Then, listening, I realised it was a wireless I could hear. I opened the front door quietly, wheeled the bicycle into the street and propped it against the wall of the house. Then I went back inside, leaving the front door fractionally ajar.

Except for the muffled murmur of the wireless and a creak from the odd stair, there wasn't a sound as I crept upstairs again. I strapped the golf-bag across my shoulders, took a last look round, switched off the light, crept downstairs and out of the house again, closing the door silently behind me. I switched on the bicycle lamps back and front, mounted and rode off.

There was little traffic about as I cycled towards Regent's Park, with a detour by way of Cumberland Terrace. I wanted another look at No.16 to make sure I had its exact location firmly fixed in my mind's eye. There was no car outside though there were two, both Daimlers, parked further along. Back into the Outer Circle and so to Regent's Park where I switched off my bicycle lamps and wheeled the machine along a path which led to the bandstand. I passed only two other people, a man walking a dog and a small boy kicking an empty tin. I propped the bicycle against the bandstand, removed the front lamp and used it to look round for a more secure hiding place. A section at the rear of the bandstand was open to the ground. I retrieved the bicycle, waited a moment to ensure that there was no one else about, then laid the bicycle on the ground and pushed it underneath the bandstand. Satisfied that it was hidden from view in the darkness, though it might well be visible in daylight, I made my way across the Broad Walk and switched on the bicycle lamp again to locate the small rear gate. It gave a faint squeak as I opened it and passed through, closing it behind me. By now my eyes had become accustomed to the darkness and I had no need of the bicycle lamp as I made my way across the damp grass. I walked along the side of the building and round the front, looking up at the scaffolding. There were lights on at some of the windows, but drawn blinds prevented anyone inside from seeing out.

It was a cold, damp night, but no fog as yet. I retraced my steps towards the rear of the building, switching on the bicycle lamp briefly in search of the ladder I had seen earlier. As I had surmised, it was still in place, still lashed to the scaffolding, its woodwork wet and cold to the touch as I climbed. The golf-bag across my back snagged on one of the supporting poles as I stepped on to the scaffolding. I manoeuvred it clear. The bicycle lamp was more of a nuisance and I decided to devise some way of suspending it about my neck when the dummy run became the real thing. Add a ball of twine to my list of purchases. Visibility was just sufficient on this occasion to enable me to negotiate the scaffolding without using the lamp, but it might be necessary another night. For the moment, I jammed it into one of the pockets of the overcoat. Cautiously, I made my way along to the front of the building. Now I had a view of Cumberland Terrace. There were lights behind drawn curtains at most of the downstairs windows. I counted the street lamps to locate No.16. The bare branches of a tree obscured my view. I moved further along the scaffolding, counted again and this time I had it. I lay down on the damp scaffold boards, my legs at an angle to my body, feet spread-eagled. There was a clear field of fire to the doorway of what I gauged to be No.16.

In the distance a church clock chimed the quarter. I stayed there until — a lifetime later, it seemed — I heard the same clock strike midnight, changing my position frequently to ward off cramp, standing up and moving around silently from time to time to restore lost circulation. The evening, as far as Cumberland Terrace was concerned, was quiet and peaceful. Occasionally a car came to or departed from a house, though not from No.16, the front door of which remained firmly closed. Cold, boredom and loss of concentration were going to be the main enemies, it seemed. I must remember the brandy tomorrow. And bring some chocolate for energy.

Tomorrow night I would have my hunting-rifle with me.

5

The Journal
(November 25-26)

I spent the following morning making my final preparations. In case Mrs Martin should see me (though she did not), I had to don my disguise of wig, glasses and second-hand overcoat to leave Toddington Crescent. But I could hardly go to my bank like that to draw money. So I had again to venture into one of those disgusting public lavatories in order to remove my disguise before hailing a taxicab to take me to the bank, the items of disguise concealed in a carrier bag. I withdrew £50 from the bank in unused white five-pound notes. Then I went shopping for a travelling alarm clock, a ball of twine and some chocolate. As an afterthought, I also bought some cigarettes, Du Maurier, and matches. I am not, have never been, an habitual smoker but there are times when I feel the need for a cigarette. I had had precious little to eat in the last thirty-six hours and was feeling more than a bit peckish. I could have done with a good tuck-in at Simpson's or the Savoy, but that carried the risk of running into someone I knew. And the last thing I wanted was to become involved in casual conversation. So I settled for a Lyons Corner House again, this time the one just off Trafalgar Square. I did myself as well as the menu permitted, soup followed by a mixed grill with cheese and biscuits and a couple of cups of coffee to conclude. Then it was through to the toilets and back into my disguise.

Mrs Martin was just leaving the house when I got back. 'Got some shopping to do,' she vouchsafed, almost grudgingly. 'Shan't be long.'

Now was my opportunity to explore. There was no telling

when I might need an emergency exit. I closed the front door and went through to the kitchen. A fire burned in a stove of blackened iron. Something was simmering away in an iron saucepan on top. There was a worn easy chair to the side of the stove. Opposite was a rain-smeared window with a brownstone sink beneath it. Beside the window was a door leading outside. I opened it and went out into a small yard. A path of grey tiles ran to a wooden gate at the bottom. The gate opened on to an alleyway. There was a wooden shed at the bottom of the yard and a brick-built bunker for holding coal immediately beneath the window of my room. Knowledge of that might come in handy if things went wrong.

I went back into the house and up to my room. I permitted myself the luxury of a single cigarette before undressing and getting into bed. I didn't imagine I would fall asleep – my mind was too alive for that – but just in case I set the travelling alarm clock for six o'clock and lay down with the wig still in place. It was as well I did so. I did fall asleep ... a nightmare occasion in which I was pursuing Mrs S through a house of endless rooms while unknown forces pursued me in turn. Another door shut ahead of me with a resounding bang ... and another beyond that. Then I realised that I was no longer asleep and the banging was not part of my nightmare. Someone was knocking on the door of the room.

It was Mrs Martin. She didn't wait for me to say 'Come in', but was already in the doorway as, struggling awake, I fumbled for the glasses to complete my disguise.

'That bike of yours. Didn't harf bark my shin on it.'

'I'm sorry,' I said.

'You'll have to keep it round the back – in the shed.'

I was about to say that it was a long way round, but checked myself in time. I wasn't supposed to know where the shed was. 'How do I get round to the shed?' I asked.

'There's an alley down the back. The number's painted on the gate.' She sniffed. 'You can pop in and out through the kitchen if you want.'

The last thing I wanted was to come and go with her sharp, beady eyes on me.

'I don't mind going right round,' I said.

'Suit yourself.' She retreated along the landing, leaving the bedroom door open behind her.

I got up and closed the door. The hands of the travelling clock pointed to half past five. I turned off the alarm, switched on the light and drew the curtains across the window. I poured some cold water from the jug into the basin and rinsed my face to dissipate the remnants of sleep. I dressed in the plus-twos and tweed jacket, slipping a flask of Courvoisier into one of the pockets and a slab of chocolate into the other. I wound my watch.

As a precautionary measure against Mrs M walking in again, I wedged the chair under the knob of the door. I cut off a length from my ball of twine and fastened it from shoulder to shoulder criss-cross fashion, knotting it in front with the ends left loose so that I could tie the bicycle lamp in place later. I put on the overcoat, lifted the mattress and brought out the Mannlicher. I checked the action of the bolt. Sweet as a nut.

The golf clubs I had used for the purpose of my dummy run came out of the bag and the Mannlicher took their place. My silk scarf, wound round the barrel, served to wedge it neatly. I unclipped the front pocket, emptied out the old score cards and tees and substituted a clip of ammunition.

I removed the chair, opened the bedroom door and listened. Silence. I tiptoed down the stairs with the golf-bag belted across my back, lifted the bicycle out into the street, closed the front door quietly behind me and set off for Regent's Park. Reaching the bandstand, I again hid the bicycle underneath, first removing the front lamp. It was a cold, damp, moonlit night.

The iron gate gave a small rusty protest as I entered the grounds of St Katherine's. There was no need of the bicycle lamp as I crossed the grass into the shadow of the scaffolding and stood there for a moment, listening. The only sounds were a car passing along the Outer Circle and the distant coughing roar of the lions in the Zoological Gardens.

I looped the loose ends of the twine through the bicycle lamp and tied it in place, leaving both hands free. The woodwork of the ladder was damp and greasy to the touch. I edged my way cautiously along the scaffolding, crouching where I had to pass the drawn blind of a lighted window. Having gained the front of the building, I eased off the golf-bag and extracted first the Mannlicher and then the clip of ammunition. The clip held five cartridges, more than sufficient. Indeed, at a range of 150 yards or so, with a street lamp affording adequate illumination of the target, I felt confident of notching up a kill with a single shot.

I settled into position, counting the street lamps to locate No.16. I drew a bead on the lighted fanlight above the door, then lowered the rifle until I had the dead centre of the door, about five feet up. Should I go for the head or the heart? Circumstances would probably settle that for me when the moment came. I relaxed and waited.

Occasionally a car passed along Cumberland Terrace. One parked in front of a neighbouring house. A man and woman came out and got in. The car pulled away. But the front door of No.16 remained obstinately closed. Somewhere a church clock struck eight. Had I been there only an hour? It seemed like ten. My concentration had gone momentarily, as I had known it must. I placed the rifle quietly beside me and sat up, wiggling my toes and fingers to restore lost circulation. I sipped a little brandy and ate a portion of chocolate. Then I took up my firing position again. Every hour I repeated the exercise.

Hunting game in Kenya had taught me patience. Your prey didn't always show up on the first night. There was one occasion on which I had to wait three nights, perched in a tree ...

I tensed as another car came along the street, slowing in front of No.16. Relax, I told myself. Tension could cause a jerk on the trigger instead of a squeeze; could mean missing the target. But the car went on past No.16 and stopped in front of the next house.

When the church clock struck midnight, I decided that enough was enough. Mrs S was not going out that night. If, indeed, she was even in the house. For all I knew, she could be at Fort Belvedere with the King. Well, there was always another night. I unloaded the rifle, replaced both it and the ammunition clip in the golf-bag and slipped the bag over my shoulders. No.16 was in darkness now except for the window of what I took to be one of the bedrooms. I retraced my way along the scaffolding, and descended the ladder. The night was darker now and I had to flick the lamp on from time to time as I made my way back to where I had hidden my bicycle.

*   *   *

Sleep did not come easily to me that night. My body was tired, but my brain was almost frenetically alive. What I needed, I told myself as I tossed and turned in that uncomfortable little bed, the

Mannlicher again safely hidden beneath the lumpy mattress, was advance information as to Mrs Simpson's comings and goings. But that sort of information was impossible to come by. Some of those who worked for her might know, her personal maid, even one of the footmen or scullery maids at 16 Cumberland Terrace, given the gossip that goes on below stairs. But there again, I had no knowledge of who worked for her and no way of contacting any of them even if I did. Then, just as I fell asleep, an idea came to me.

Like most ideas which come on the verge of sleep, it looked less promising the following morning by the grey light of another misty November day. But it was still worth a try. So I spent a large part of the morning walking the streets in the vicinity of Cumberland Terrace. The public house I was seeking was further off than I had hoped for, but it was the nearest there was. If any of the Cumberland Terrace servants slipped out for a spot of liquid refreshment, this was the establishment they would make for. I went into the saloon bar. There were only a few other people in the bar, two or three men and a solitary woman, stout and red-faced. A cheerless fire burned in a small grate.

There was a high-backed settle each side of the fireplace, one largely occupied by the stout, red-faced woman. I ordered a glass of port and sat down opposite her.

'Cold day,' I observed.

' 'Tis that.'

'You live near here?' I asked.

'Near enough. I can tell you don't.'

'How's that?'

'The way you talk – posh-like.'

'I work round here,' I said, untruthfully. 'In Cumberland Terrace.'

'Ah,' she said, leaning forward. 'That's where she lives, ain't it?'

'You mean Mrs Simpson?'

'That's her. You work for her?'

'No,' I said.

She lowered her voice to a hoarse, confidential whisper. 'They say as how the King visits her there.'

Her glass was empty. 'What are you drinking?' I asked.

'Mother's ruin.'

It sounded like one of the Pink Flamingo's cocktails, but I couldn't imagine cocktails being served in a place like this. 'Let me get you another,' I said. 'Mother's what was it?'

'Ruin – gin to you.'

I went over to the bar. 'Could I have another gin for the lady near the fire.'

The landlord, a tall, grey-haired man, grinned. 'Caught you for one, has she? That's Flo for you.' He poured a generous measure of gin into a glass. Two of the men in the bar had taken advantage of my move to occupy the settle on which I had been sitting and the fat woman moved up a bit to make room for me beside her. 'Ta, duckie,' she said, taking a big gulp of the gin.

'You were telling me about the King calling on Mrs Simpson,' I prompted her.

'Common knowledge round these parts.' She leaned across to the two men. 'Ain't it, Fred?'

'Ain't it wot, Flo?'

'Common knowledge. About the King coming to Cumberland Terrace.'

'Oh, that.' He was a small, wizened ferret of a man with crafty eyes. He switched his glance from Flo to me. 'God's strewth. Got it from the bloke wot works there.'

'What bloke is that?' I asked.

'Dunno his name. He's in here most days.'

At that moment the door opened and another man came in.

'Him?' I asked.

He shook his head. 'No – nothing like.'

'What time does he usually come in?'

His eyes took on a suspicious look. 'You ain't one of those reporters, are you?'

I shook my head in turn. 'Works in Cumberland Terrace,' Flo volunteered for me.

'That's all right then. Comes in about one-ish usually.'

But not that day he didn't, though I remained in the saloon bar until closing time, buying more drinks for Flo, for the two men and for myself. I also bought myself a couple of sandwiches. The drink-buying integrated me into the small clique of regulars. 'Any chance that he'll be in tonight?' I asked the ferret-faced man as we emerged, Flo swaying somewhat, into the damp greyness of the outside world.

'Who's that?'

'Him who works for Mrs Simpson.'

'Dunno for sure,' he said. 'Might be, I reckon.'

While I could not possibly be in two places at once, I did not have to be an Einstein to work out a way of reducing the time-factor between the two as much as possible. To do this necessitated leaving Toddington Crescent some three-quarters of an hour earlier than on the previous evening, the Mannlicher in my golf-bag. I made my way along the street and back along the rear alleyway to where my bicycle was now housed in the tumbledown shed. I belted on the golf-bag and pushed the bicycle to the end of the alley before switching on the lights and mounting it.

I cycled to the bandstand in Regent's Park, but had to wait while a courting couple finished their billing and cooing before I could secrete the golf-bag under the bandstand. Then I cycled back to the public house I had visited at lunch time.

Except for its swinging sign, it might have been no more than an ordinary house in a terrace of ordinary houses. In fact, it had probably once been two such ordinary houses which had later been knocked into one. There was nowhere to leave the bicycle except against the wall. I propped it under the lighted window of red and blue glass which carried the legend Saloon Bar, decided that in that position it represented an open invitation to any sneak thief who might come along, and moved it further along into the shadows where it was less noticeable.

Apart from the landlord, there was only one other person in the saloon bar, the ferret-faced man of earlier acquaintance.

'Thought you might be in,' he said, screwing up one eye in what was apparently intended to be a conspiratorial wink.

'What are you drinking?' I invited.

What was left in his glass disappeared down his throat in a twinkling. 'Don't mind if I do,' he said. 'Mine's an old and mild.'

I had no idea what an 'old and mild' was, but the landlord did and the glass was re-filled. I ordered myself a small brandy.

The ferret-faced man was staring at me in curious fashion.

'That a wig you're wearing?' he asked.

There was no point in denying it. I had to think fast. 'Yes,' I said. 'I suffer from alopecia.'

'Alo-what? Never heard of it. Have you heard of it, George?' he asked the landlord.

'Can't say that I have.'

'It causes your hair to fall out,' I explained.

'Ain't catching, is it?'

'No,' I said, laughing. 'It isn't catching.'

'Thank Gawd for that.'

I felt a cold draught as the outside door opened behind me. The ferret-faced man gave me another ponderous wink and jerked his shoulder. 'That's him,' he whispered, masking his mouth with his glass of old and mild. I turned towards the newcomer and bade him good evening.

'Evening,' he returned, unbuttoning his mackintosh. He was youngish with a pale face, full lips and plastered-down hair.

'Buy you a drink?' I offered.

'Don't mind if you do. Whisky and ginger, please, George.' The landlord served him and he raised the glass in acknowledgement. 'Skin off your nose.' He sipped his drink. 'This won't buy you anything, you know. Reporter, aren't you?'

The ferret-faced man came to my rescue. 'You're wrong there, mate. Works where you do – Cumberland Terrace.'

'That so?' he looked at me, his eyes wary. 'Who for?'

I said the first name that came into my head. 'Mrs Curtis-Manners.' It was the name of one of my aunts, though she did not reside in Cumberland Terrace. 'I only started there this week,' I lied.

'Thought I hadn't seen you in here before.'

'You're at No.16 aren't you?' I asked, trying to sound diffident.

'How'd you know that?'

'From me,' chipped in the ferret-faced man. He was proving a useful, if unwitting, ally.

'Don't wonder you're wary of reporters,' I said. 'I'd be the same if I were in your shoes.'

The landlord folded his arms and leaned on the bar. 'So what's going on at No.16?'

'Nothing special.' But the grin accompanying the remark suggested that he knew more than he was willing to reveal.

It was Fred of the ferret face who turned the key to unlock Pandora's box. He had probably never heard of psychology any more than he had heard of alopecia, but he knew how to apply it. 'Take no notice of him,' he sniffed. 'He's just trying to act big. He don't know nuffin.'

His needling had the desired effect. 'Don't know nothing, don't I? Well, I know this much. I know his nibs is coming to dinner.'

The way he said 'his nibs', almost capitalising the two words, could mean only one person. I decided to take a leaf out of Fred's book.

'Go on,' I said. 'Pull the other one. Trying to make out the King is coming to No.16.'

'Who said anything about the King?'

'Just like I said,' interjected Fred. 'Just trying to look big.'

'That's not fair,' I said, playing my part. 'If the King's dining at No.16 tonight, he's quite right to keep it secret.'

'Tomorrow night,' said the young man.

'Well, tomorrow night then. That why you've got tonight off?' I asked.

'No such luck. Just popped out for a quick one.' He fished a watch from the pocket of his waistcoat. 'Got to be getting back.' He finished his drink. 'Ta-ta all.'

'I've got to get back too,' I said. 'I'll come with you.'

I tried to find out more as we walked together through the lamp-lit streets, but it was no good. Either he genuinely didn't know or he wasn't saying. It was only as we neared Cumberland Terrace that I realised that I had prepared a trap for myself. He was going to want to know at which house I worked.

'Heavens,' I said, stopping.

'What's wrong?'

'I've just remembered. I've left my bicycle outside the public house. I must dash back and get it. See you another night, I hope.' And, turning, I walked quickly away.

The bicycle was still where I had left it. I turned on the lights, mounted it and rode towards Regent's Park. I dismounted once I reached the park, switched off the lights and pushed the bicycle towards the bandstand.

I leaned the bicycle against the bandstand, knelt in the damp grass and felt underneath for the golf-bag. A sudden sense of apprehension seized me as I failed to find it. Someone must have seen me hide it, pulled it out again, found the Mannlicher, sent for the police. At any second I expected to feel a heavy hand on my shoulder and hear a gruff voice say, 'Better come quietly'.

When nothing happened, I stood up, took the lamp from the bicycle, knelt again and, screening the beam of light with the overcoat, looked again under the bandstand. The golf-bag was about a foot to the right of where I had been fumbling. I dragged it out and hid the bicycle in its place. Ten minutes later I was in position on the scaffolding and gazing along the sights of the rifle at the front door of No.16. I still had no knowledge of whether or not Mrs S was going out that evening. If she did, the chances were that she would climb straight into a waiting car. I would have only a second or so at most. Best if I had what is known in the army as 'one up the spout'. I had already clipped the magazine of the rifle into position. Now, quietly, gently, I operated the bolt of the Mannlicher to bring the first round into firing-position.

* * *

I had been there just over half an hour – somewhere a church clock had struck the quarters twice – when a car slid to a standstill in front of No.16. A man got out of the front of the car and I followed him through my sights as he went towards the front door.

Then, suddenly I was bathed in light. Someone had switched on a light in the room immediately behind and slightly above me, its yellowness drawing a metallic glint from the barrel of the Mannlicher. At all costs I must not panic. Whoever was in the room would almost certainly come to the window to draw the blind. Once that was done, I was safe again. Meanwhile, if I remained quite still, I would perhaps go unobserved. Lying there, my back to the lighted window, I felt intensely vulnerable. It was a temptation to look round. But I knew I must not move.

For a second or so nothing further happened. Then there was a rapping sound as of knuckles on glass. Now I had to look round. There was a figure at the window, silhouetted against the light behind. Man or woman I could not tell. Wood rasped against wood as the window opened. 'You out there – what do you think you're doing?' A man's voice.

I started to come to my feet. My foot slipped on the damp planking. With my left hand I grabbed at the nearest scaffold pole to prevent myself from falling. For a split second my right hand was forced to take the full weight of the rifle, my finger still on the trigger. Involuntarily my hand tightened its grip and the rifle went off.

'Christ!' said the voice behind me.

The figure at the window disappeared and I heard shouting. Recovering my balance, I slipped the Mannlicher into the golf-bag and made my way back along the scaffolding. There was more shouting, this time from beneath me. Running feet scuffed the gravel path which circled the building. The beam of a flashlamp traversed the scaffolding.

I had rounded the corner of the building when I heard another sound. Someone was climbing the ladder. My retreat was cut off. I turned and retraced my original route. My eyes had long since become accustomed to the greyness of the night. Ducking, I made my way past the open, lighted window which had been my undoing to where the brickwork of the building turned outwards at right angles. Here the scaffolding ended.

An almost vertical ladder led upwards to the second tier of scaffolding above me. I scrambled up it. Pursuing feet made their way along the planking below. The moon had risen and the slate tiles of the roof gleamed dully in the moonlight. The roof ran in two directions and between the two angles of the roof a leaded gulley sloped upwards.

I belted on the golf-bag so that both hands were free, climbed on to a cross-pole of the scaffolding and hoisted myself on to the roof. I crouched for a moment on the angled slope, then pushed myself upright and, leaning forward to maintain my balance, scuttled upwards. I had almost made it to the top when my feet slipped under me. Just in time I grabbed at the ridge tiles and hung there, panting. From below came the voices and running feet of those pursuing me.

My breathing almost back to normal, though my heart was still racing, I hauled myself up until I could see over the ridge. On the far side four areas of roof descended at different angles to form a hidden valley. I climbed over the ridge and slid down another leaded slope. Then I made my way along the valley of lead and slates towards the rear of the building.

Now more confident of my roof-climbing ability, I ran up another of the angled slopes and clung to another ridge while I surveyed the area beyond. Below and ahead of me I could see the lamps of Regent's Park. There were no sounds other than those natural to the night. The hunt for me seemed to be concentrated at the front, the occasional shout muted by the intervening roof.

Immediately below me a leaded gulley sloped down to where the roof ended two storeys above the ground. Try sliding down that and it could end in disaster. A few inches at a time, lying flat against the slope of the roof, hand following hand, I worked my way along the ridge until I reached the far end. I levered myself up and took another look. Another leaded gulley sloped down to a stout chimney stack with another roof below. I climbed over the ridge and began a descent of the gulley, slowly and cautiously, on my feet, bottom and hands, the lower end of the golf-bag, weighed down by the butt of the Mannlicher, bumping against the slates as I went. My feet skidded under me at one point, but the drag of the overcoat checked my slide.

I felt for the guttering with my feet, testing it for stoutness before letting it take my full weight, squatting against the slope to take a breather, my shoulder against the brickwork of the chimney stack.

A few inches at a time, I raised myself to a standing position, before turning, little by little, until the chimney stack was in front of me. The guttering sagged under me. Quickly I stretched one leg round the corner of the stack in the direction of the lower roof. Unbalanced, I felt myself swaying slightly. But now I had no choice. My changed centre of gravity would not permit me to recover my original balance and I made the enforced jump.

I landed on my hands and knees, momentum causing me to slide down the slates of the lower roof. I prayed that there was another gutter at the bottom to bring me to a halt.

There was. I lay on the roof, face down, my feet resting on the gutter. Now, if I had gauged things correctly, I was surely no more than ten feet above the ground at most. But even that drop could result in a broken leg if I fell awkwardly.

I worked my feet along the guttering until another wall checked my progress. Unable to turn my head to see it properly, I explored it with one hand. My hand touched something colder and of different texture from the brickwork. I judged that it was a large, square-shaped drainpipe designed to convey rainwater from a higher roof level. I secured a hold on it and pulled myself round until I could grip it with both hands. I stayed like that for a few moments, listening. There was no sound from those searching for me. Carefully, as quietly as possible, I began to climb down.

Crouching, I made my way through a shrubbery in what I

judged was the direction of Regent's Park. I found the gate without difficulty. Looking back, I caught the flash of lights as the search for me went on towards the front of the building. My hands felt sore and tender and my whole body ached as I retrieved my bicycle from beneath the bandstand. It was only when I was safe in my room that I realised that I had lost the silk scarf which I had used to wedge the Mannlicher tight inside the golf-bag.

6

Scotland Yard Investigates
(November 26-28)

Purely by chance the bullet accidentally discharged from the Mannlicher-Schoenauer hunting-rifle shattered one of the windows of No.16 and continued on its way to embed itself in the plaster of the wall opposite. The room was empty at the time, but the sound of breaking glass brought servants quickly on the scene. The possibility that the breakage had been caused by a bullet did not occur to anyone and it was reported to Mrs Simpson that someone had thrown a stone through the window. But coming on top of a succession of anonymous letters she had received, some of them threatening, even this was sufficient to alarm her.

She was in her boudoir, seated at her writing desk, when the incident was reported to her. Her first thought was of the King's visit planned for the following evening. 'Is there much mess?' she asked in that Maryland accent which so fascinated the King.

Very little, she was told. Should it be cleared up, she was asked, or left for the police to see?

The police? The thought that they might have to be involved had not previously occurred to her. It was a further complication.

'Leave it for the moment. I'll let you know,' she said.

Alone again, she stood up and took a few turns up and down the room. Normally a calm and confident woman, completely sure of herself, she was beginning to feel frightened. The anonymous letters, several of them in the same hand and bearing the same postmark, were bad enough. Now this.

She sat down again at the desk and drew the candlestick telephone towards her. The number she gave the operator was that of Fort Belvedere.

If Mrs Simpson was frightened, the King, that evening, was a man on the horns of a dilemma. The previous day he had had yet another session with his Prime Minister, their stormiest meeting so far. The King had summoned Baldwin to ask if he had given further consideration to the proposal for a morganatic marriage.

'Yes, Sir I have,' Baldwin told him, 'and it is my considered opinion that Parliament would not approve. There are also the Dominions[1] to consider. Any such marriage would require their consent also. If I may say so, Sir, you are embarking on a course which could split the Empire. And think too of the lady. The public could turn against her. Popular though you yourself undoubtedly are, your popularity might not serve to protect her.'

'Prime Minister, you forget yourself,' the King said, sharply.

'Believe me, Sir, I speak only in your own interest and that of the lady.'

Silence had fallen between them. It was Baldwin who broke it, asking, 'Am I to take it, Sir, that you wish me to examine the proposition formally? That is, to place it before the Cabinet?'

If there was a note of warning in the way he said it, the King either did not recognize it or declined to heed it.

'Yes, Prime Minister,' he said, impatiently. 'I do.'

Baldwin picked up his hat. 'Very well, Sir. I will convene a special Cabinet meeting for Friday.'

Friday was now tomorrow and the King, as he sat at dinner with two of his most loyal supporters, was becoming increasingly and uncomfortably aware that by insisting that Baldwin should raise the possibility of a morganatic marriage formally in Cabinet he had, in the words of one of his two guests, put 'his head on the chopping block.'

It was Lord Beaverbrook, the dynamic gnome-like Canadian-born proprietor of the influential *Express* newspaper group, who had used the expression. He had been aboard the liner *Bremen* in mid-Atlantic, en route for his native Canada, when a radio-telephone call from the King had urged his return. There was increasing danger that London's newspapers would not much longer maintain their self-imposed silence concerning the King's companion and Beaverbrook's presence in London could do much to ensure that some at least of the newspaper comment was favourable to the King's cause.

Now, over dinner, stabbing the air with his knife to emphasize his points, Beaverbrook quickly elaborated his 'chopping-block' theme. 'Sir, you are placing your future in the hands of the politicians. You are bound to do whatever the Cabinet decides. If you do not, the Government will immediately resign as lacking Your Majesty's confidence.'

'The Cabinet may decide in my favour.'

Beaverbrook shook his head. 'Not if Baldwin has anything to do with it.'

The King turned to his other guest, Walter Monckton[2], a friend since their university days and perhaps the most brilliant barrister of his day, the man he had first consulted about Wallis Simpson's divorce.

'What do you think, Walter?'

The barrister pondered the point for a moment, then said, 'I must agree with Lord Beaverbrook.'

'You must telephone Baldwin, Sir,' said Beaverbrook. 'Tell him you have changed your mind. Say that you no longer wish the Cabinet to consider the proposal.'

'Is that your view too, Walter?' the King asked.

Before Monckton could reply there was a tap on the door and a footman entered. He approached to where the King was sitting, bent over and murmured in his ear. The King removed his table napkin from his lap and placed it on the table. 'If you will excuse me, gentlemen. There is a telephone call.'

The King went through to the library and picked up the telephone. 'What is it, Wallis?'

The voice in his ear was not the firm, slightly domi-neering one to which he was accustomed. For once she sounded upset, distraught. 'Thank goodness you're there, David. It's so frightening. Someone has just thrown a stone through the drawing-room window.'

'You're all right, Wallis?' Concern for her showed in the King's voice. 'You're not hurt?'

'No, David. The drawing-room was empty at the time. But a stone through the window. It makes you wonder what's next.'

'Don't distress yourself. It was probably an accident. Some boys larking about.'

'You can't believe that, David. Not after all those terrible letters I've been receiving.'

'I've told you, Wallis – they're the work of cranks. I'm coming to dinner tomorrow night. We'll talk about it then.'

'Can't you come tonight, David?'

'It's awkward, Wallis dearest. I'm entertaining guests.'

'Are they important guests?'

'Walter Monckton and Beaverbrook. We're discussing the morganatic marriage proposal. They think I should drop it.'

'David, you mustn't.'

'The Cabinet could turn it down.'

'Why would they do that? And even if they did, we're simply back where we were. No worse off.'

'We could be.'

'How could we be, David? I don't understand.'

'It's difficult to explain. It's a matter of the constitution.'

'Don't listen to them, David. I'm sure it's the right way.' She no longer sounded distressed, but her customary rather hectoring self. 'You go back in there and make them see our – your – point of view. You are the King, David.'

'Tell you what I'll do, Wallis. I'll get Evans[3] to come there right away. He'll look after you. And he can arrange for a constable to be stationed outside the house. That will stop any more stone-throwing. And don't worry about those silly letters. They're just cranks letting off steam.'

'Oh, thank you, David. Just talking to you has made me feel so much better.'

True to his word, the King sent immediately for Inspector Evans and gave him the necessary instructions. Only when that was done did he rejoin his guests in the dining-room. 'I've been thinking over what you said, Beaverbrook,' he told the newspaper baron, 'and I have decided to let the morganatic marriage proposal stand.'

As the King bent again over his plate, Beaverbrook and Monckton looked at each other, both faces reflecting their doubts and anxiety. And both men sensed that the King's decision was not his own, but that of Mrs Simpson.

It was some twelve hours later, just after breakfast the following morning, when the King was informed that Chief Superintendent Sinclair had arrived at the Fort and desired to see him. 'Sinclair?' he murmured, puzzled. 'Oh, very well. Show him in.'

Sinclair entered, a well-built middle-aged man with immensely shaggy eyebrows. It was the first time he had met the King and he was concerned to conduct himself properly. He inclined his head in a polite bow and murmured, 'Good morning, Your Majesty.'

'Morning, Superintendent Sinclair.'

'Chief Superintendent, Your Majesty. Your Majesty –'

'Sir will suffice, Chief Superintendent.'

'As you say, Your Majesty – Sir. Sir, I am here as a result of an incident at No.16 Cumberland Terrace, the residence of Mrs Simpson.'

'I know about that. Someone threw a stone through her window.'

'No, Sir.'

The King looked momentarily baffled. 'Someone didn't throw a stone through her window?' he queried.

'No, Sir. Not a stone and it wasn't thrown. It was a bullet, Sir, and it came from a gun.'

'Good God. You mean someone tried to kill her?'

'I don't know, Sir. If so, it was a pretty rotten shot. It was fired into an empty room. Mrs Simpson was nowhere near at the time.'

'You've got the man who did it?'

'I'm afraid not, Sir.'

'He got away?'

'Yes, Sir.'

'And he is still at large?'

'Yes, Sir.'

'Free to try again?'

'It remains a possibility.'

The King paced up and down for a moment.

'Mrs Simpson must be protected at all costs. She is a friend of mine.'

'I understand, Sir. Steps have already been taken. I have had a constable posted at the front door and have assigned detectives to pursue the case energetically.'

'You've no idea who the man is?'

'Not for the moment, Sir. We are following up various leads, in particular threatening letters Mrs Simpson has been receiving.'

'I thought they were the work of some crank.'

'Cranks have been known to resort to violence, Sir. Mrs Simpson received a letter this morning. That makes six in the same handwriting. They're being tested for fingerprints at the moment.'

'Good. That should find the villain for you.'

'Possibly, Sir, but I am not inclined to expect too much in that direction.'

'Why not?'

'Fingerprints can be identified only if we already have them on file, Sir. Safe-crackers, burglars and such-like. If our man isn't one of those, he won't be on record.'

'I see.'

'It is my understanding, Sir, that you were planning to have dinner at Mrs Simpson's this evening.'

'I am.'

'With respect, Sir, I would advise against it. In fact, I have already taken the liberty of saying so to Mrs Simpson.'

'Have you, indeed?'

The Scotland Yard man could feel himself sweating. But he ploughed doggedly on. 'Yes, Sir. I understand that she has decided to cancel the dinner party.'

'On your advice, Chief Superintendent?'

'In a manner of speaking – yes, Sir. And I have

instructed Inspector Evans to resume duty with you later today.'

The King's brow contracted. 'Mrs Simpson's safety must come first.'

'No, Sir. With respect, it is your own safety that must come first.'

The King sniffed audibly. 'No one's going to harm me.'

'I will see to it that Mrs Simpson is given a suitable replacement, of course.'

'Perhaps it would be safer if Mrs Simpson left Cumberland Terrace altogether,' the King suggested.

'An excellent idea, Sir. Have you any suggestion as to where she might go? An hotel would not be advisable. Too many comings and goings.'

'She would come here, of course.'

'To Fort Belvedere, Sir?'

'Yes. Why not?'

From the gossip which was going round about the King and 'the King's companion', Chief Superintendent Sinclair could think of one excellent reason why not. But it was not for him to say so. As though reading his thoughts, the King smiled. 'I would ensure that the lady is properly chaperoned.'

'Of course, Sir,' Sinclair said. 'If those are your wishes, I will make the necessary arrangements.'

'No need, Chief Superintendent. I will make them myself.'

His unexpected visitor gone, the King seated himself at his desk and drew a sheet of notepaper towards him.

Darling (he wrote), *You could be in danger*.

The rest was brief and to the point. He would send a car for her as soon as it was dark. She should be packed and ready. She should let no one know where she was going. *People talk*, the note concluded.

The King sealed the letter, addressed the envelope, rang for his chauffeur and instructed him to deliver it forthwith. Much safer than a telephone call, he thought. Telephone calls involved operators and who could tell what they might chance to overhear.

Mrs Simpson was still in bed, her secretary seated at the

bedside, going through her morning mail, when the King's note reached her. 'Leave me,' she said, pushing the rest of the mail aside, 'but send my maid to me. I must get dressed. And ask my aunt to come and see me.'

She was at her dressing-table when her aunt, Bessie Merryman, a stout little body, bustled into the room.

'Aunt Bessie. Start packing immediately. We are going away.'

'Now – this instant?'

'Tonight.'

'Am I permitted to ask where we're going?'

'You are not. But I'll give you a clue.' She looked across to where the maid was laying out her clothes for the day; lowered her voice. 'You will be acting as chaperon.'

'You mean we're going to the –'

Wallis brought a finger to her lips. 'Shhh.'

A mile or so to the south, as the maid hauled out suitcases, hat boxes, shoe boxes and Mrs Simpson instructed her what to pack, the Prime Minister was meeting with members of the Cabinet at No.10 Downing Street. The King's desire to contract a morganatic marriage with Mrs Simpson now being formally tabled, it was the cabinet's duty to consider it. The meeting did not last long. Almost all present were opposed to the idea and the one or two who may not have been, kept their thoughts to themselves. From Baldwin's preliminary soundings, it seemed a foregone conclusion that the Dominions would take the same line. But the proposition having been formally tabled, they had to be formally consulted. Draft wordings for the messages to be sent to them were circulated and approved, and with them the King's fate was sealed, though it would be a few more days yet before that became apparent.

At Scotland Yard at roughly the same time, Chief Superintendent Sinclair was going through the available evidence which might – though he was not very hopeful – lead him to whoever had taken a pot-shot at the drawing-room window of 16 Cumberland Terrace. He knew, from the report of a subordinate, that the shot had almost certainly come from the scaffolding of the building opposite Cumberland Terrace. Ballistics had identified the bullet dug out of the drawing-room plaster as 6.5 mm which meant that it was probably from an Italian-made rifle, either a military Mannlicher-Careano or a Mannlicher-Schoenauer, the sporting version. Other rifles of the period, Britain's Lee-Enfield, the German Mauser and the American Springfield, used different gauges of ammunition.

The anonymous letters received by Mrs Simpson had yielded a liberal supply of prints which Fingerprints were trying to match up, a long and tedious process. Sinclair did not have much hope in that direction. The letters were more likely to have been penned by unknown cranks than recorded villains. And even if a set of fingerprints could be identified there was no guarantee that letter-writer and marksman were one and the same.

There remained one other possible clue, a silk scarf found on the ground beneath the scaffolding. It had seemed at first to Sinclair that it had probably fluttered down from an open window, but inquiries so far had failed to turn up anyone who laid claim to it. So it was just as well, he thought, that he had sent it along to Forensics. Now he had the scarf back, on the desk in front of him, together with the forensic report. The report noted that one side of the scarf suggested that it had been trodden underfoot with an analysis of the mark revealing a mixture of soil, leaf mould and small grit. A smear on the other side had been identified as having been made by a light oil that might have come from something like a bicycle or rifle.

Sinclair studied the scarf intently. White silk. The sort sported by dashing young men in their flying machines. Also by young men who rode high-powered motor-cycles or zipped around in snazzy little sports cars. It looked newish; not a cleaning rag. Made in Italy. Trademark: *Garibaldi*.

He leaned over to flick the lever on the intercom which connected him with his civilian secretary. 'Ask Detective Sergeant Thompson to come to my office, please.'

A few minutes later there was a tap on the door and Thompson entered. 'You sent for me, sir?'

Young and clean-cut, Thompson was a product of the not-long-established Police College at Hendon, university educated, a copper of the new school. There were some at the Yard who tended to resent newcomers from Hendon, classing them as jumped-up young jackanapes, too clever for their own good. Not so Sinclair. He saw sense in the policy of taking young men of above-average intelligence and giving them special grooming in police work. Thompson, in particular, he considered to be not only highly intelligent, but hard-working and ambitious if perhaps a little inclined to cut the occasional corner.

'Take a look at that, sergeant,' he said, indicating the scarf.

Thompson picked it up. 'Silk scarf, sir. Been trodden on.' He studied the label as his superior had done. 'Made in Italy. Could have been brought back from holiday.'

Of course. Sinclair had not yet thought of that, though the possibility would probably have dawned on him later. If so, then it was a dead duck.

'Possibly,' he said. 'Also possible that it was bought here. See if you can find out whether anyone imports that particular make of scarf. Then get a list of shops that stock them. Then see me.'

'Am I permitted to know something of the background, sir? You never know, it might help.'

'Last night someone put a bullet through a window in Cumberland Terrace.'

'I heard about that,' said Thompson. 'Home of a very special lady, I hear.'

Sinclair looked at him quizzically. 'News travels fast, it seems. What else have you heard?'

'Only that – ' Thompson checked himself. He had been going to say, 'Only that she's the King's mistress.' He thought better of it and added, ' – she's a friend of the King's.'

'So you know to tread carefully,' said Sinclair. 'That scarf was found near the spot from which the shot was fired. There's a smear of oil on it. On the other side, see. Could be rifle oil. Of course, it's always possible that there is no connection between the scarf and the shooting.

Could be that you're on a wild-goose chase. But it's also possible that that scarf will see us home and dry before there's another try at popping off Mrs Simpson. Or anyone else. So make a thorough job of it.'

Thompson had handled other enquiries in similar vein during his so far comparatively short time at the Yard and knew how to go about things. First, he made a telephone call to the Italian Embassy, asking to be put through to the commercial attaché. The commercial attaché spoke excellent English. 'I will look into the matter and call you back,' he said.

Less than an hour later Thompson had the telephone number of the clothing manufacturing concern in Milan which used the *Garibaldi* trademark. But the resulting telephone call to Milan was fraught with complications.

'I want to speak to the sales manager,' said Thompson.

'Chi parla?' queried a female voice at the other end.

Thompson raised his voice a few decibels and spaced out his words. 'The – sales – manager – please.'

The reply was a string of words, fast and incomprehensible. Thompson pressed the mouthpiece against his chest. 'Anyone here know Italian?' he demanded of those around him. He sighed and shouted again into the mouthpiece, 'The – sales – manager.'

This time there was no reply. He could hear voices in the background and the clacking of a typewriter. 'Are – you – there?' he demanded, loudly.

Another voice came on the line, male this time. 'What you want?'

Thompson sighed with relief. 'I want to speak to the sales manager.'

'Not here.'

'The general manager then.'

'He speak no English.'

'Does the – sales manager – speak – English?' Thompson asked, slowly and deliberately.

'A little.'

'What – time – will he – be there?'

The background was filled with a volley of excited chatter. Then the man's voice said, 'You call four o'clock.'

And with that Thompson had to be content. At four o'clock he called again. This time, after only a few minutes of delay and confusion, he found himself connected to a Signor Umberto whose English was sufficient for him to understand who Thompson was and what he wanted. A few minutes later he had the name, address and telephone number of a firm of wholesale distributors in London's Commercial Road. He called them and found himself speaking to the proprietor's secretary. She was sorry, she said, but Mr Sikorski had gone for the weekend. Thompson explained what he wanted. Sorry, she said again, but she could not divulge such information without Mr Sikorski's authority. Thompson asked for Mr Sikorski's telephone number. She was sorry again, but she could not give it.

'This is Scotland Yard,' Thompson insisted. 'This is a police inquiry.'

'On the telephone anyone can say they are the police.' Her voice had a nasal intonation.

Thompson knew how to handle that. 'True,' he said. 'You can't be too careful. Tell you what – I'll hang up and you call Scotland Yard – Whitehall 1212. Ask for me – Detective Sergeant Thompson.'

'All right.'

She sounded doubtful, but the call came within minutes. She would still not give him the information herself, but was prepared to surrender Mr Sikorski's private number in Golders Green.

Mr Sikorski, when Thompson got on to him, was inclined to be petulant. He had only just reached home. Wasn't a man entitled to a little privacy? The information Thompson wanted was at his office. It was a long way back. Finally, reluctantly, he agreed to meet Thompson at the premises of Sikorski Fashions at seven o'clock.

The detective's visit was still an hour in the future when a chauffeur-driven Daimler glided to a halt outside the entrance to 16 Cumberland Terrace, where a uniformed constable now stood guard. A solitary figure occupied the rear compartment and remained there, face in shadows, while the chauffeur spoke briefly to the constable and then went to the front door of the house. The door opened and, between them, the chauffeur and a footman brought out a quantity of luggage, so much of it that some had to be accommodated beside the chauffeur on the front seat of the car.

That done, the small plump figure of Mrs Merryman emerged from the house, closely followed by the taller, slimmer figure of her niece. Only then did the man in the rear compartment emerge into the November gloom. As the light of the nearby street lamp illuminated his features the uniformed constable gave a quick gulp and a flustered salute. He had never thought he would be that close to the King. Something to tell the missus when he got home.

The King helped Mrs Merryman into the rear compartment. Then he embraced Wallis Simpson briefly and decorously, murmured something the constable failed to hear, and helped her in also. The King himself climbed back into the car and the chauffeur slid back behind the steering-wheel. The constable saluted again, more smartly this time, as the Daimler drew smoothly away.

Long after the King, his companion and her Aunt Bessie had arrived at Fort Belvedere that evening detectives in a dozen towns and cities throughout Britain continued their inquiries. They were not given the reason for such inquiries and had little to go on. They knew only that someone high up had been sent an anonymous and threatening letter postmarked in their area. Not surprisingly, their inquiries produced no results.

The report from Fingerprints, which reached Chief Superintendent Sinclair the following day, was likewise negative. Not one of the prints lifted from the various anonymous letters received by Mrs Simpson could be matched in the Yard's voluminous files.

Only one slight hope remained. Detective Sergeant Thompson had returned from Sikorski Fashions with a pile of old shoe-boxes. The silk scarves imported from Italy had been sold by mail order and the shoe boxes contained the order forms. He had had the good sense to impound them and Sinclair had realized immediately the possibility of matching up the handwriting on one of the order forms with that of at least one of the anonymous letters.

There had been a delay in starting work on this because the letters were still with Fingerprints. But once Fingerprints had finished with them, two teams of detectives, one under Thompson, the other in the charge of Detective Sergeant Blunt, an experienced, tenacious copper of the old school not far from retirement age, had been put to work. They sat at trestle tables, each with one of the anonymous letters in front of him (excluding the few posted in the United States and Canada) while the order forms were passed in turn from man to man.

There were several thousand order forms clipped from various newspapers – the scarves had been advertised at six shillings and elevenpence each or £2 for half a dozen – and the work of checking and comparing went on late into the evening with Thompson or Blunt called over from time to time to check a possible match. Chief Superintendent Sinclair telephoned his wife to say that he would not be home for supper and remained in his office while the checking went on. Big Ben had chimed eleven o'clock before the last comparison had been made and the two teams of detectives could finally relax, stretching cramped limbs and rubbing tired eyes. Thompson and Blunt looked at each other in disappointment.

'No joy, old son,' said Blunt.

Thompson nodded dejectedly. 'Better go tell the Old Man.'

Chief Superintendent's long years at the Yard had made him well accustomed to such disappointments. He knew now that it would require an extraordinary stroke of luck to lead him to whoever had fired that shot through Mrs Simpson's window.

7

The Journal
(November 29-30)

It was lunchtime on Sunday before I discovered that Mrs S was no longer at Cumberland Terrace. Which meant that all my efforts towards finding a new firing-point since my rooftop escape on Thursday night had been wasted.

My whole body had felt one big ache when I awoke on Friday morning. My hands and knees were badly grazed and there were bruises on my arms, thighs, abdomen and parts of my body which I could not see. What I needed was a good long soak in the tub.

I had not taken a bath since moving to Toddington Crescent. Normally it is my custom to bathe once and sometimes twice a day, though going without was no hardship. I had done it before when on safari and my stalking of Mrs S was by way of being another safari. I had been put off taking a bath at Toddington Crescent by a combination of factors: the bathroom's slightly unpleasant odour, the minor explosion when one turned on the gas fitment which delivered the hot water and the fact that there was no way to lock the bathroom door. I didn't want Mrs Martin popping in and catching me in the raw. And certainly not that Friday morning when my naked body looked as though I had gone ten rounds with James J. Braddock.[1]

So I waited until I heard her go out before hurrying along to the bathroom, turning on the potentially lethal gas fitment, filling the bath and climbing in. The hot water did something to ease my bruised and aching body. Epsom salts would have helped, but I didn't have any.

I was out of the bath, dressed and enjoying a cup of coffee when

Mrs Martin returned. I heard her go through to the kitchen, emerge again a few minutes later and stump up the stairs. Without knocking, she opened the door of my room.

'You bin having a bath?' she demanded.

'Yes,' I said.

'You shouldn't take a bath without telling me first.'

She extended a hand. 'That'll be a tanner.'

I found sixpence and gave it to her. 'What have you done to your face?' she asked.

There was a graze on my left cheekbone. 'Fell off my bicycle,' I lied.

Later that morning I made my way back to Cumberland Terrace, leaving my bicycle behind. Walking would give me a chance to see more; find out what was going on. To my surprise there was a uniformed policeman stationed outside the door of No.16 and nearby a small group of men in raincoats and trilbies. Several of them had cameras of the professional kind. Newspaper photographers. Further off was another small group of people, mainly women. I joined this second group.

'What's going on?' I asked.

It was one of the women who answered me. 'It's her as is mucking around with the King,' she said in a working-class voice. 'Someone bunged a brick through her window last night.'

'Thought I heard one of those newspaper blokes say it was a bullet,' a man chipped in.

'Someone tried to do for her, you mean?' the woman asked.

'Looks that way.'

'Good riddance to bad rubbish, if you ask me,' said another woman.

I knew it must be the bullet I had accidentally discharged in making my escape which had shattered the window of No.16.

'Police any idea who did it?' I asked.

'Search me,' said the man. 'There's some of them poking about over the road; at St Katherine's.'

I walked back to the Outer Circle and along to the gates of St Katherine's. Inside the grounds some half-dozen bobbies were walking across the grass in line abreast, heads down as though looking for something. The bricklayers were working away on their scaffolding as usual. There was also a man in a raincoat on the scaffolding, moving slowly along its length. He too appeared to be *looking for something.*

They could hardly be searching for my scarf. Only I knew that I had lost it in the course of making my escape. And even if they found it, it would tell them nothing. There were hundreds of scarves about just like it. Well, dozens. And I hadn't even bought this one myself. It had been a birthday gift.

My narrow escape had done nothing to weaken my resolve. I was still determined to kill Mrs Simpson. But now things were clearly going to be more difficult. There was a policeman outside No.16 and likely enough there would be one guarding the scaffolding come nightfall. Which meant finding another firing-point.

On Saturday I had reconnoitred the area again. There was no longer a policeman on duty outside No.16 and the newspaper photographers were down to two. But the crowd of onlookers had doubled or trebled in size and the mood had turned ugly. There were shouts of 'Get back where you belong' and 'We don't want you here' and others which were downright obscene. I hoped Mrs S could hear them.

It was just after midday and the builders at St Katherine's appeared to be packing up for the weekend. I saw them unlash the ladder which led to the topmost run of the scaffolding and carry it away round the corner of the building. No doubt, on police orders, they were going to do the same with the lower ladder. Presently they appeared again round the corner of the building, pushing a small handcart from which their ladders projected fore and aft. There was now no way in which I could gain access to the scaffolding. I moved round the outskirts of the crowd, still shouting their offensive remarks, my eyes seeking an alternative firing-point. There was a church, but that was on the same side of the road as No.16. The angle of fire would be too acute. That left only St Katherine's itself. I wondered if there was perhaps an empty room overlooking Cumberland Terrace.

Then, on Sunday, I discovered that my bird had flown.

* * *

I had gone to the public house that lunch time in the hope of again seeing the young manservant from No.16. My luck was in and I entered the saloon bar to find him standing in front of the fire, glass in hand. Behind him, on the wall above the fireplace, hung a picture of the King – the old King who had died at the beginning of the year. Fred and Flo were there too, seated opposite each other on the two settles. Flo was as near the fire as she could get, her skirt pulled up to her knees and her fat legs apart. I ordered a glass of port and a sandwich and moved over to join them.

'Haint seen you for a few days,' said Flo.

'I've been busy,' I said, perching myself on one of the settles.

'Don't they feed you at your place?' asked the manservant.

'The sandwich, you mean,' I said, shrugging. 'Got up too late for breakfast.'

He was dressed as though for a day off, a shiny navy-blue suit with a blue polka-dot tie. A matching polka-dot handkerchief dangled from his breast-pocket. His shoes were highly polished and his hair neatly slicked.

'Where did you say you worked?'

'Mrs Curtis-Manners,' *I lied, again taking my aunt's name in vain.*

'All right, is she?'

'Not bad,' I said. 'Could be worse. This your day off?'

'Nothing to do,' he replied.

'Away for the weekend, is she?'

'Something like that.' *He was still cautious – cagey – but his very caution told me something.*

'Gone back to America, has she?'

'Not America,' he said.

Not America. Where then? Out of the country? Had the King given her up? I hoped so. If so, my task was at an end. But if not, I would have to start all over again. How to find out where she had gone? I could hardly ask outright.

Fortunately, Flo had no such inhibition.

'Where's she gorn then? Go on – you're among friends. You can tell us.'

'My lips are sealed.'

Fred joined in, falling back on well tried tactics. 'If you ask me, you don't know. Your kind are all the same – allus trying to act big.'

'You don't catch me that way,' said the young man. 'I do know and I can prove it. Where she's gone there's a turret.'

'What's a turret?' Flo asked.

'A sort of tower,' I explained. I looked at the manservant. 'Isn't it?'

He nodded. 'From which you can see the scenery,' he said, cryptically. 'Any the wiser?' he asked. He finished his drink and set his glass on the mantelpiece. 'Well, I'm off.'

The door of the bar closed behind him. 'What's he mean?' Flo asked, petulantly. 'What's scenery got to do with it?'

'He don't know where she's gorn,' said Fred. 'That's the truth of it.'

But he did know. And now I knew too. He had made a mistake in classing me with Fred and Flo. He might baffle them, but I knew what he knew – that a turret overlooking scenery is called a belvedere. His cryptic allusion had been to the King's country home. That's where Mrs S had gone. And not just for the weekend, it seemed.

I knew very little about Fort Belvedere. I knew, of course, that it was on the fringe of Windsor Great Park, about five miles from Windsor Castle. I'd seen pictures of it. A strange-looking place with towers and battlements and rusty cannon. Not really a castle, though built to look like one long after the need for castles had gone. Castle or not, it afforded Mrs S a secure haven so long as she remained within its walls. But sometime, surely, she must come out again.

I returned to Toddington Cresent and lay on my bed, thinking. Windsor was over twenty miles from London. I could hardly bicycle there. I had a car, but using it was out of question. It would be too easily identified. Yet I would need some form of transport to reconnoitre the area. And then it came to me.

* * *

It was shortly after nine the following morning when I left Toddington Crescent. I would probably need more money. I still had most of the fifty pounds I had drawn from the bank, but it might not be enough. The bank did not open its doors until ten o'clock, but I had other things to do first. I found the sort of shop I wanted in Euston Road. Disguised in the long coat and red wig, I went in and bought a set of black leathers together with a leather helmet, goggles and lace-up boots. I packed all this in a haversack which I also bought.

My next call was at a public lavatory where I divested myself of the coat, wig and glasses, packing them into a paper carrier bag I had brought with me. Looking myself, I took a taxi to the bank where I drew out another hundred pounds. Another taxi took me to Fortnum & Mason where I asked them to make me up a picnic basket for one. They packed me some nice fresh rolls, a pat of butter, a breast of chicken, a portion of French cheese, some fruit and a quarter-bottle of champers. I hailed another taxi to take me to the station where I purchased a first-class return ticket to Windsor.

There were few people on the train at that time of morning and I had no difficulty getting a compartment to myself. The train had no corridor and I was able to change into my newly acquired leathers in privacy. I had thought to wear the wig and glasses as a disguise, but found it impossible to don the leather helmet without disarranging the wig and was forced to settle for just the glasses. Later, I would change them for the goggles, but not yet. I folded the clothes I had been wearing and packed them, along with the overcoat and wig, into the haversack.

At Windsor I found the sort of place I was looking for in one of the side-streets opposite the castle. It was a workshop in which a youngish man, grease on his face, was performing surgery on the entrails of a motor car. 'No good you asking,' he said before I had asked anything. 'Up to my neck. Can't take on anything else until next week at least.'

'I want to buy a motor-cycle,' I said.

'That's different.' He straightened up and wiped his hand on an oily rag. 'I suppose you can ride one?'

'I'd hardly be buying one if I couldn't.'

In fact, I had been riding motor-cycles, on private roads and around fields, since I was twelve, though I had never actually owned one. They had belonged to my brother; well, half-brother actually.

The garageman led me outside to where some five or six machines were lined up. 'Take your pick,' he said.

But while I could ride a motor-cycle, that was about the limit of my knowledge. 'Which do you recommend?' I asked.

He wandered along the row of machines, giving a pat here and a tap there rather as though they were horses. 'If it was me, I'd go for the Norton,' he said, finally. 'Good enough for the Isle of Man T.T. she is.'

'How much?'

He named a figure. 'I'll take it,' I said.

He was so surprised at this that he offered 'to fill her up with juice' free of charge and fetched a can of petrol from the workshop for this purpose. 'You won't have no trouble with her,' he said, 'but come back and see me if you do.'

We went back into the workshop and I counted out the money. 'There's just one thing,' I said. 'I need somewhere to keep it.'

'Keep it here if you like.'

'What time do you shut?' I asked.

'Six-ish if things are slack. More like nine this week.'

'I might be later than that,' I said.

'How about renting a garage then? There's some down the side.'

I followed him out to a yard flanked with lock-up garages. He tugged open a door. 'This one's empty. Three and six a week.'

I said I would take it for a month.

'I'll find you a padlock for the door. And the yard's open all night, so you won't have no trouble.' Like Mrs Martin, he had a fondness for double negatives.

He unearthed a rusty padlock and key from an old Sarony cigarette tin filled with odds and bits and I gave him a month's rent in return. 'Better come and see she starts all right,' he offered.

A couple of kick-starts on his part brought the Norton to life. As far as I could judge, the engine ticked over smoothly enough. I slipped my arms through the shoulder straps of the haversack, fixed my picnic hamper to the carrier at the back, removed my unnecessary spectacles, donned the goggles and climbed into the saddle. The support bracket sprang up with a clatter and I was off, wobbling a little.

I spent the next hour or so exploring the area around Fort Belvedere. There was a group of men in mackintoshes and trilby hats outside the main entrance. Newspaper reporters, I guessed, with a uniformed constable on duty to keep them from trespassing. The countryside around was well wooded. I found a quiet spot, ran the Norton off the road and wheeled it a few yards further until it was well hidden. Then I made my way on foot through the trees until I came to a stone wall. A tree close to the wall enabled me to see over. Beyond it, only a few trees and ornamental shrubs separated the wall from an open area where the drive from the main entrance swept round to the front of the house. I had found my firing-point.

I climbed down and retraced my steps. My motor-cycle was where I had left it, propped against a tree. I sat on the saddle and ate my picnic lunch while I thought things out. Mrs S was hardly likely to be walking about the grounds after dark. Which meant that the deed would have to be done in daylight. But I would have to scale the wall and take up a position close to the house under cover of darkness.

My meal finished, I tore one of the empty Fortnum & Mason paper bags into small strips and used them to lay a paperchase trail through the trees. I spiked one piece of paper to a low branch; another into the torn bark of a tree-trunk. Others I left on the ground among the dead leaves, fixing them in position with broken pieces of twig stuck into the damp peat-mould. Satisfied, I pushed the motor-bicycle back on to the road, got it going after half a dozen kick-starts and rode back into Windsor.

While I didn't relish the idea of spending the next few days and nights out in the open, particularly at this time of year, there was compensation in the fact that I could abandon the tedious business of changing my appearance so frequently. But for the time being I had to change it yet again for the benefit of Mrs Martin. I had hoped to effect the change on the train from Windsor and to this end again obtained a first-class compartment. But at the last moment two other people, a man and a woman, got in. In consequence, when the train steamed into London, I had again to lock myself in the cubicle of a public lavatory before returning to Toddington Crescent.

I dumped the haversack at the foot of the stairs, walked along the hallway and tapped on the door of the kitchen. Mrs Martin opened the door. The kitchen was clouded in steam and had a smell of cabbage.

'I have to go away for a few days,' I told her. Some sort of explanation was required and I had given careful thought as to what it should be. 'I don't know how long I'll be gone,' I said. 'My father's seriously ill and I'm his only living relative. I have to be there.'

'Sorry about your father,' she said. It was the first truly human remark I had heard her make.

'I'd like you to keep the room for me,' I said.

Her next remark was more her usual form. 'You haven't paid this week's rent yet.'

'I know. I'll pay this week and next.' I gave her the money.

I retrieved the haversack and went upstairs to my room. I rolled back the mattress, picked up the Mannlicher and put it in the golf-bag with the clubs around to conceal it. Then I dragged the suitcase from under the bed and jammed the haversack into it together with such items of grocery as would come in useful. But not the tea or coffee. I wasn't going to light any fires which might betray my presence. But I would need something to drink. A further shopping expedition was necessary.

There was a newsagents a short walk away which seemed to sell almost everything under the sun, a small dark shop crowded with groceries, newspapers, cigarettes, sweets and hardware. I bought a bottle of lemonade – I could have done with two or three bottles, but weight was a consideration – together with some bars of chocolate, cigarettes and matches, tins of corned beef, sardines and tomato soup, the only variety of soup available. The soup would have to be consumed cold but I could hardly afford to be choosey. From a nearby off-licence I bought a half-bottle of cognac. I carried my haul back to Toddington Crescent and stowed it in the suitcase. On a further shopping foray, to Euston Road this time, I purchased a sleeping-bag. Nights out of doors in England in November were going to be rather different from those spent previously in Kenya. That evening I went out for the last solid meal I was likely to enjoy for several days.

It was between nine and ten when I got back to Toddington Crescent. A light on upstairs showed that Mrs Martin had already retired for the night, though she was not yet asleep. I let myself into the house as quietly as possible and tiptoed upstairs. She must have had ears like a hawk. Light flooded the landing as she opened her bedroom door and stood there in a shapeless flannel night-gown.

'I'm off now,' I said. 'Just come back for my things.'

'How you're going to get there this time o' night?' she asked.

'There's a late train,' I said, which was no more than the truth. I had checked the timetable on my way back from Windsor and planned to catch the last train.

There was no question of a taxi in the immediate vicinity and I had to walk to the taxi rank in Euston Road. It was just before midnight when I reached Windsor. The suitcase seemed heavier than ever as I walked to the lock-up garage. It had no electricity and I changed into my motor-cycling gear by the light of the flashlamp. I strapped the golf-bag across my back. That left the problem of how to convey the suitcase. The Norton was equipped with a carrier but I had overlooked the need for something with which to fasten the suitcase in place. A hunt round the garage solved the problem and a length of electrical wiring served the purpose.

Despite my good sense of direction, I lost my way twice before reaching Fort Belvedere. When I finally got there I wheeled the motor-cycle off the road and hid it among the trees. I left the suitcase hidden with it after first transferring the sleeping-bag, the bottle of lemonade and some of the other items to the haversack. With the haversack on my back and the golf-bag over one shoulder, I used the flashlamp to follow my paper trail to the wall. Laden as I was, scaling the tree was more difficult than on the previous occasion. I straddled the wall and dropped down on the other side. My first task was to make sure of an escape route. I put down the golf-bag and explored my surroundings, screening the beam of the flashlamp with my hand. I had gone perhaps twenty or thirty yards when I came to a supporting buttress, its stonework in a sufficient state of disrepair to provide handhold and foothold. I used my knife to cut a strip of bark from a low branch to serve as a marker.

I retrieved the golf-bag and made my way slowly and cautiously through the trees in the direction of the house. A light still on in one of the upstairs rooms served as a guiding star. Satisfied, I retraced my steps, removed the haversack, got out the sleeping-bag, wriggled into it and settled down for what remained of the night.

I did not sleep well, dozing off only to jerk awake again perhaps a few minutes, perhaps an hour, later. The night was full of rustlings and scufflings. Somewhere a dog fox barked. Despite the sleeping-bag, the ground felt hard and I twisted and turned uncomfortably. A longer period of uneasy sleep ended with the twittering of birds. The blackness of the night had turned to greyness. It was time to be up and doing.

I folded the sleeping-bag and returned it to the haversack. I *made myself a meal of biscuits and corned beef, drank a little lemonade, and took a sip of cognac. I drew the Mannlicher from the golf-bag and inserted a clip of ammunition. I put some more biscuits, chocolate and the half-bottle of cognac in the pockets of my leathers. I covered the haversack and golf-bag with leaves. Then I again made my way through the trees in the direction of the house.*

The trees ended in a patch of mown grass. There was a bed of earth from which sprouted a mass of rhododendrons. I slipped across the patch of grass and burrowed into them. Through their foliage I had a clear view of the drive and entrance. Now it remained only for Mrs S to emerge from the front door. I settled down to wait.

8

A Vital Lead
(December 1-2)

Mrs Martin climbed awkwardly out of bed, stretched, yawned, pulled her off-white flannel nightdress over her head, dropped it on the floor and sat down again on the bed, scratching her belly. While she scratched, she thought. All this coming and going late at night. That was queer. And that red hair. She'd lay a level quid it was a wig. Put the two together and it suggested something shady, that's what.

Once before Mrs Martin had had a dodgy lodger. Three years ago that was and that was the sentence he had been given: Three years' hard labour. For burglary. She herself had nearly been charged with receiving stolen property. All on account of a wireless she had bought from him. Only the fact that the police couldn't prove she *knew* the wireless was nicked had prevented her ending up in court. Well, she hadn't known, had she? Not actually *known*. She didn't want more trouble, with that all raked up again. Best, if there was anything shady going on, if she went to the police first.

She dressed and plodded along the landing to the room occupied by her absent lodger. She switched on the light and looked round. Nothing there that shouldn't be. She knelt down and looked under the bed. Nothing there either. She was straightening up again when something caught her eye. She bent again to retrieve it. It was a small piece of thin white card headed Royal Blackmere Golf

Club. There was a name written on it in pencil. It was not the name of her lodger.

She went down to her small, stuffy, smelly kitchen and brewed herself a pot of tea. She poured herself out a cup, added milk and three heaped teaspoons of sugar, stirred it vigorously and drank it thoughtfully. As well as wearing a wig – and all those night-time comings and goings – it looked as though the lodger was also using an alias. Or was it an alibi? All very dodgy. Best way to keep her own nose clean was to go to the coppers before they came to her. But suppose everything was on the up-and-up? Then involving the police could mean losing a lodger who stumped up on the nail and without question.

Well, there was one way to find out whether those night-time comings and goings were fishy or not. Mrs Martin finished her tea, put on her hat and coat and went out, plodding flatfooted in the direction of St Katherine's. Reaching the main entrance, she pushed through the swing doors.

She tapped on the glass panel labelled 'Inquiries'. It slid back to reveal a seemingly disembodied head from which the hair was drawn back tightly into a bun. Impatient eyes regarded her through a pair of pince-nez. 'Yes, what is it?' the woman demanded in a querulous voice.

'I've come to see my lodger,' Mrs Martin said.

'Visiting hours six to eight,' the woman retorted, sharply.

Mrs Martin shook her head. 'Ain't a patient. Works 'ere.'

'Why didn't you say so then. What name?'

'Davis.'

'Medical, administrative or domestic?'

Baffled by so many long words, Mrs Martin had to think for a moment. 'Paperwork,' she said finally.

'Wait a minute.' The glass panel banged shut.

It was fully five minutes before it opened again and the woman said, 'There's no one of that name here.'

So I was right, Mrs Martin thought. But she had to be sure. 'Gone on holiday?' she queried.

'I told you, didn't I? There's no one by the name of Davis works here.'

'Ta ever so,' said Mrs Martin, adding under her breath as

she walked away, 'old bitch.'

Her mind was made up. She would go home again, have a bite to eat, then go to the cop-shop. However, she was saved the necessity for doing so by an encounter with Police Constable Nobbs. He was standing in a shop doorway, engaged in a little bend and stretch exercise designed to relieve his aching legs.

'Mornin', ma,' he said, affably.

'Mornin', Mr Nobbs,' said Mrs Martin. 'Just the man I wanted to see.'

They had known each other by name since that day, three years ago, when Nobbs had drunk tea in her kitchen while a detective constable searched the lodger's room upstairs.

Nobbs sighed good-humouredly. He was accustomed to being 'just the man' people wanted to see, when they had lost a dog, found a bicycle pump, been locked out by their wives, been knocked about by their husbands or wanted someone to scare the living daylights out of little Willy for using foul language. 'What is it, ma?' he asked.

'I ain't sure,' said Mrs Martin. 'But I don't like it.' And she told him about her curious lodger.

'Better get this down,' the constable said. He unbuttoned the breast pocket of his tunic and brought out a notebook and pencil. he licked the lead of the pencil. 'Name?' he asked.

'You know my name,' said Mrs Martin.

'So I do.' Nobbs wrote in his book. 'Address?'

'You've been there.'

'So I have. Toddington Crescent, isn't it?' Mrs Martin nodded. 'What number?' She refreshed his memory.

Nobbs continued writing. 'Gave the name of Davis, but you think it's false.'

' 'Tain't the name on this,' said Mrs Martin, producing the golf score-card.

'I'd better take possession of that,' said Nobbs. 'Claims to work at St Katherine's, but doesn't. Goes out a lot at night. Comes back late. Wears a wig.'

'I only think it's a wig. A red one.'

Back at the police station, Nobbs reported his conversation with Mrs Martin to the duty sergeant who told him to put it on paper and passed the resulting rather ungrammatical report to the inspector in charge. The inspector detailed a detective constable to have a further word with Mrs Martin. The detective, a youngster named Henderson with less than three months' experience, was conscientious in the extreme. After questioning Mrs Martin to an extent which half filled his notebook, he went upstairs to inspect the lodger's room, Mrs Martin trailing at his heels.

Henderson proceeded round the room, carefully noting down the lodger's few possessions. Then he embarked upon a more thorough search, lifting up the mattress to see if there was anything underneath, reversing the sampler which hung on the wall in case anything had been taped to the back, climbing on the chair to feel along the top of the picture rail, getting down on hands and knees to crawl around the room.

An exclamation escaped him. 'You got such a thing as a pair of tweezers?' he asked Mrs Martin.

'No,' she said.

'An old envelope?' Henderson asked.

'I might have.'

She trudged downstairs and came back with a creased and crumpled envelope bearing the imprint of the local rating office. Henderson used the blade of his penknife to flick his find clear of the skirting, picked it up between the penknife and a pencil, and popped it into the envelope.

Back at the police station, Henderson wrote out his report and passed it, together with his find, to the inspector. The inspector sent it, together with the golf score-card and the report of P.C. Nobbs, to Scotland Yard. And it was there, the following morning, that the file landed on the cluttered desk of Detective Sergeant Blunt. Blunt knew a 6.5 mm bullet when he saw one. He also knew that it was a 6.5 bullet which had been dug out of the plasterwork at 16 Cumberland Terrace. He went over to the large street map of inner London which covered one wall and studied the relationship between Cumberland Terrace and Toddington Crescent, then decided that this was something that should be brought to the attention of the Chief Super.

He replaced the various items in the file and carried the file along to the Chief Superintendent's office where he found himself having to wait because Sinclair already had someone with him. The 'someone' was a member of the Special Branch whose latest report had added considerably to the Chief Superintendent's worries.

'This crowd got a name?' he asked the Special Branch man.

'Empire Royalists they call themselves, sir.'

'And there's talk of a bomb?'

'Yes, sir.'

'With Mrs Simpson as the target?'[1]

'Without doubt, sir.'

'They plan to plant it where?'

'Don't know, sir.'

'Well you'd better find out.'

'That could take a little time, sir. I have to be careful not to arouse suspicion.'

'To the devil with that,' Sinclair said, heatedly for him. 'We don't have much time. You know who these so-called Empire Royalists are?'

'Two or three. Not all of them, sir.'

'Well, pull those two or three in. Separately.'

'On what charge, sir?'

'I don't care what charge. Anything will do. But separately, you understand. Then grill them. We must know where they plan to plant their confounded bomb.'

The Special Branch man went out and the Chief Superintendent's secretary popped her head round the door. 'Sergeant Blunt to see you, sir.'

'Blunt? What's he want?' The question was rhetorical. 'Give me a couple of minutes, will you?'

Sinclair needed time to think. It was one thing if these Empire Royalists thought that Mrs Simpson was still at Cumberland Terrace; quite another if they knew she was now at Fort Belvedere. Didn't want a bomb going off at either place, of course, but Fort Belvedere, with the King there also, was by far the more important. Should he tell the King? He looked at his watch. Give it till this afternoon. Special Branch might have found out more by then.

The door opened. 'Sergeant Blunt, sir.'

'Yes, Blunt, what is it?'

Blunt told him.

'Let's have a look at the file, sergeant.'

Sinclair skimmed quickly through the reports of Police Constable Nobbs and Detective Constable Henderson. He lifted the flap of the envelope and peered inside.

'Haven't touched it, have you?'

'No, sir.'

'Right. Let's get it along to Fingerprints. Tell my secretary to come in.'

Blunt did so and Sinclair gave the necessary instructions. The bullet on its way to Fingerprints, he turned his attention to the score-card. 'Not much good sending this to Fingerprints. Everyone under the sun seems to have handled it – the beat constable – that landlady – what's her name?' He referred again to the reports. 'Mrs Martin. The lodger gave her the name of Davis. But that's not the name on the card. Could have been left there by someone else.'

'It's this present lodger who has a set of golf clubs, sir.'

'Royal Blackmere, eh? Played there myself once. Rather a lot of trees. Wonder who the secretary is.'

The secretary turned out to be a Colonel Logan. Sinclair's face changed noticeably as he listened to what the club secretary had to say. For several minutes after replacing the telephone he sat in silence. When he finally spoke he said, 'Now we really are treading on eggshells, sergeant. The name on that card is the heir to a dukedom – a marquess no less. Lives in Buckinghamshire. A member of the Royal Blackmere, though he hardly ever plays there.'

'But he can't be the person who lodged with that Mrs Martin. The description –'

'No,' Sinclair interrupted him. His mind went back to the so-called Empire Royalists and their bomb plot. 'But there could be more than one. He's got to be seen, but it's got to be done carefully. I suppose I ought to go myself.' He looked again at his watch. Should be there and back by lunch time or a little after. Still plenty of time to go further into the bomb business and see the King if necessary. He picked up the telephone again and asked for his car to be brought round. 'You'd better come with me, sergeant.'

The house was a smallish but elegant Elizabethan structure set in parkland. A herd of deer grazed in the park and ancient oaks overhung the drive. A butler answered the door. There was a wait of some minutes before the Chief Superintendent and his sergeant were shown into the library where a log fire crackled and spluttered cheerfully. The Duke's heir stood in front of the fire, a pleasant-faced man with fair hair. Around thirty, give or take a couple of years, Sinclair judged.

'And to what do I owe the honour of a visit from Scotland Yard?' he asked, smiling. 'Whatever it is, I didn't do it.'

I'm quite sure you didn't –' Sinclair broke off, unsure whether to address him as 'sir', 'my lord' or what.

'Drink?' asked the Marquess.

A good idea, thought Blunt, but the Chief Superintendent, having decided on 'my lord', said, 'No, thank you, my lord.'

'Forget the formality,' said the Marquess. 'Sit down. Might as well make ourselves comfortable.' They sat. 'Now what can I do for you gentlemen?'

'I believe you are a member of the Royal Blackmere Golf Club,' said Sinclair.

'Am I? Yes, I believe I am. Haven't played there for at least two or three years though. What's this all about, Chief Superintendent?'

'In a moment, sir. Is this yours?' Sinclair passed over the score-card.

'I suppose so. That's my name on it and looks like my writing. Yes, I remember. I was spending a weekend at the ancestral seat and we played a round there. My wife and I against my sister and some boyfriend. Where did you get it from?'

'It was found in a house in Toddington Crescent.'

'Where's that?'

'In London. Not far from Cumberland Terrace.' Sinclair brought the name in deliberately, hoping for some reaction.

'I know Cumberland Terrace, of course. Near Regent's Park. But I've never heard of Toddington Crescent. Can't imagine how this got there.' The score card was passed back.

'You been there recently, sir?' Sinclair asked.

'I told you. I've never even heard of Toddington Crescent. As for Cumberland Terrace, I went there once to a dinner party.'

'Was the dinner party at No.16 by any chance?'

'Hanged if I know. It was years ago.'

'And you haven't been there since?'

'No.'

'Mind telling me where you were last Thursday evening, sir?'

'Last Thursday? Just a tick.' The Marquess stood up, went over to his desk and flicked over the pages of a large leather-bound diary. 'Ah, here it is. Thursday. Meeting of the local Conservative Association, seven thirty pip emma.'

'And the meeting finished at what time, sir?'

'Nine-ish. Nine thirty.'

Could still have been in Cumberland Terrace time enough to have taken a pot-shot at the window of No.16, Sinclair thought. 'Do you have a gun, sir?' he asked.

'Several, Chief Superintendent. A brace of Purdeys, a hunting-rifle.'

'What make of rifle?'

'Mannlicher.'

'Six point five millimetre?'

'Yes. Really, Chief Superintendent, you might tell me what all this is about.'

'All in good time, sir. You left the Conservative meeting about nine or nine thirty, you say.'

'No, Chief Superintendent, I did not say that.' The Marquess was suddenly less good-humoured. 'You asked me when the meeting ended and that was what I told you. I stayed on for another hour at least. I'm the chairman.'

'Anyone else stay on with you?'

'Yes, of course. The secretary and a couple of members of the committee.'

'If I could have their names and addresses.'

'Of course.' The Marquess was still standing at his desk. He picked up a gold fountain pen, wrote quickly and jerkily on a pad, tore off the sheet on which he had written and thrust it across at the Chief Superintendent.

'Thank you, my lord.'

Sinclair stood up and Blunt did the same. 'Just one thing more,' Sinclair said. 'Do you possess such a thing as a white silk scarf?'

The library door opened at that moment and the heir's wife entered. 'Oh, I'm so sorry,' she apologised. 'I didn't know you were engaged, darling.'

'Quite all right,' said the Marquess, stiffly. 'They're just leaving.'

'About that scarf,' Sinclair prompted him.

'What scarf is that?' asked the Marchioness.

'They want to know if I have a white silk scarf,' said her husband. 'Do I?'

'Two, darling. I bought them for you. Bought half a dozen, in fact.'

Sinclair looked at her, wondering if she too could handle a hunting-rifle. With the change in her husband's mood from good-humoured banter to controlled anger, he did not dare ask. But he was determined to pursue the subject of the scarves.

'What happened to the other four, your ladyship?'

'The other four what?'

'Silk scarves, your ladyship. You said you bought half a dozen and gave two to your husband. I was wondering what happened to the other four.'

'I've still got them. I haven't –' She checked herself. 'Silly of me. I gave two away as a present.'

'Do you mind telling me who to, your ladyship?'

Her husband said, 'Lydia, I don't think –' His intervention came too late. The Marchioness had already mentioned a name. The Marquess said, rather sharply, 'I wish you hadn't told them that. Until we know what this is all about, I don't think we should have involved anyone else.'

'Sorry, darling,' the Marchioness said in a low voice.

The Marquess frowned in Sinclair's direction. 'I really must insist that you tell us the reason for all these questions, Chief Superintendent. Are we suspected of something?'

'Of course not, my lord,' Sinclair said, soothingly. He needed an address – and a photograph – but the situation had become far too sensitive to ask for either. As it was, the husband at least was likely to be on the telephone as soon as he and Blunt had left. A lie might help. 'It's all a bit silly really, but we have to follow these things up. It's just that someone's been taking pot-shots at animals in the Zoological Gardens.'

'How unkind,' said the Marchioness.

'No one in our family would do a stupid thing like that,' said her husband. 'It's ridiculous to think it.'

'Quite ridiculous, my lord,' Sinclair agreed. 'I can assure you I am quite satisfied,' he lied.

On which note, followed by a baffled Sergeant Blunt, he made good his escape before either the Marquess or Marchioness could think to ask how a white silk scarf came to be involved.

Back at Scotland Yard, Sinclair gave his civilian secretary the name the Marchioness had let slip and asked her to track down an address and telephone number. *Who's Who* listed two addresses, one in London, the other in the country. Furnished with these, Sinclair summoned Detective Sergeant Thompson. Blunt was a good enough detective, but lacked the finesse that might be needed in making further inquiries.

'I want you to call that number,' he instructed Thompson, 'and ask for that person. If you don't get them there, try the other number.'

'And if I do get them, sir?'

'That's where you have to box clever, sergeant. Have a good plausible excuse for your telephone call. Nothing to do with the Yard, of course. Don't want to startle our fox. Then let me know immediately.'

'I understand, sir.'

'One thing more, sergeant. If you draw blank – and I rather think you will – we'll be needing a photograph. I suggest you try the *Tatler, Illustrated London News* and other publications of that ilk. One or other of them should be able to help.'

9

Flight To France
(December 2–4)

Until that Wednesday the King knew nothing of the Bishop of Bradford, and the Bishop, in turn, knew little if anything of the lady known as 'the King's companion'. His address to the diocesan conference the previous day, as he sought to assure everyone when the furore erupted, had nothing to do with Mrs Simpson, but was directed solely at the fact that the new King was not following in the church-going footsteps of his dead father. But the leading provincial newspapers, principally the *Manchester Guardian* and the *Yorkshire Post*, thought otherwise and seized upon the Bishop's words to break the self-imposed silence of the British press concerning the King's intentions.

In commending the King to God's grace – 'which he will so abundantly need' – the Bishop added, 'We hope he is aware of his need. Some of us wish that he gave more positive signs of his awareness.'

The King read the Bishop's words, and the construction the newspaper put on them, with a mounting sense of anger and dismay. He flung the newspaper from him. 'They don't want me,' he said, flatly.

'Yes, they do, darling,' Wallis Simpson encouraged him. 'Take no notice of the newspapers. It's the people who count. The people love you. You must appeal to the people.'

'How?' the King asked.

'Speak to them. Broadcast over the wireless. Like your

father always did at Christmas. Like President Roosevelt does in his Fireside Chats.'

'Baldwin will never permit it.'

'You must stand up to him, David. Insist. After all, you are the King.'

'I'll put it to him,' the King said, though without real conviction. 'I am seeing him again this afternoon.'

'About what?' Wallis asked.

'The idea of a morganatic marriage.'

'I thought you'd told him you no longer wished to proceed with that.'

'I did. I sent Monckton to tell him, but he told Monckton it was too late. Cables had already gone off to the Dominions. He said it could be withdrawn now only if I renounced all intention of marrying you. And that I cannot do, Wallis.'

He spoke with sincerity. But his last few words did nothing to soften the impact of the rest. 'Really, David,' Wallis Simpson said, petulantly, 'you let Baldwin push you around too much. You'd think he was the King.'

When King and Prime Minister met again, late that afternoon at Buckingham Palace, Baldwin came straight to the point.

'Sir,' he said, 'replies concerning your wish to contract a morganatic marriage have been received from the Dominions. I have the cables with me.' He placed them on the King's desk. 'You will see, Sir, that they are unanimous in rejecting any such idea. Lyons[1] is especially forthright.'

The King leafed through the cables despondently. 'I might have expected that,' he commented. 'Roman Catholic, isn't he?'

Baldwin did not reply. Instead, he said, 'You can hardly proceed against such a weight of public opinion, Sir.'

'Public opinion lies with the people, Prime Minister.'

'Indeed it does, Sir. But those cables are from men elected to represent public opinion – as I do here, Sir.'

It was an opportunity, the King thought, to broach Wallis Simpson's idea. 'I would like to know what the people themselves think, Prime Minister.'

'But you do, Sir. Those cables, the cabinet – they are unanimously against your proposed marriage. So, I am assured by Clement Attlee, is the Labour Party.'

'They are not the people, Prime Minister. It is the people who should be heard.'

'But how can that be done, Sir?'

'I would like to broadcast to them, Prime Minister.'

For the moment Baldwin was taken aback and there was a brief pause before he said, 'That would be unconstitutional, Sir. I could not permit it.'

The King's temper flared. 'You could not –' He bit it off and had himself under control again.

Baldwin corrected himself. 'I'm sorry, Sir. I should have said that I could not advise it.'

'Of course not, Prime Minister.' The King sounded bitter, though it was no more than he had expected. 'And you are my Prime Minister and I am constitutionally bound to act on your advice.'

Baldwin remained silent. 'So what is your advice, Prime Minister?' the King asked.

'Sir, I urge you again to give up this proposal of marriage. It is part of the price you have to pay because you are King. A King is not like other men. And a King's wife is not like other wives. A King's wife is also the Queen and in the choice of a Queen the voice of the people must be heard.'

'But they are not being heard,' the King muttered.

Baldwin ignored the remark, saying, 'Neither your Government here nor the Dominions will accept Mrs Simpson as Queen or, indeed, as the King's wife.'

'I still intend to marry her,' the King insisted, stubbornly.

'Sir, you must either give her up or abdicate.'

The King smiled, but it was a smile without any humour to it. 'I have known that all along, Prime Minister.'

The King arrived back at Fort Belvedere that evening to be told that Chief Superintendent Sinclair was waiting to see him. He received him in the library. 'Yes, what is it, Chief Superintendent?' he asked, eager to get the interview over so that he could see Wallis and talk with her about his encounter with Baldwin. 'Caught the miscreant yet?'

'Not yet, Sir.' Sinclair knew that the King was referring to the shot which had shattered Mrs Simpson's window. 'I am here because our inquiries have turned up something else – a bomb plot, Sir.'

'Against me?' The King was genuinely amazed. 'Impossible. You can't mean it.'

'Against Mrs Simpson, Sir.'

'I rely upon you to foil it, Chief Superintendent.'

'I am doing everything possible, Sir.'

'No harm must come to Wallis.' The King would not normally have spoken of Mrs Simpson in that fashion except to a close friend, but Sinclair's news had caused him to become overwrought. 'You must arrest those responsible before they can act.'

'We have arrested some of them, Sir,' Sinclair told him, 'but not all. We don't yet know who the others are. And we may yet have to release those arrested. We do not have the evidence to bring them to court.'

'But good Lord, man – a bomb –'

'Knowing and proving are two different things, Sir. We know they're plotting against Mrs Simpson. But we could never prove it in court. And, whether the bomb actually exists and, if so, where is it, we don't know.'

'Then what do you suggest, Chief Superintendent?'

Sinclair's primary concern was for the King's safety. The only real danger to the King was that he might be caught in a bomb blast intended for Mrs Simpson. But if he could be separated from Mrs Simpson …

It would be useless, he sensed, to put it to the King in that fashion. It had to be phrased differently; very carefully.

'In my opinion, Sir,' he said, slowly, 'Mrs Simpson's safety could best be assured if she went abroad without further delay.'

The King looked at him sharply. The words had an oddly familiar ring. Then he remembered. Alec Hardinge[2] had used much the same words in the letter he had written to the King following Mrs Simpson's divorce. '*The*

*one step which holds out any prospect of avoiding this dangerous
situation is for Mrs Simpson to go abroad without delay.'* At the
time the King had reacted angrily, angrily enough to have
thought of dismissing Hardinge. He had not done so, but
neither had he spoken to him since.

Now the crisis that Hardinge had foreseen was actually
upon him and he hardly knew which way to turn. When
Hardinge had suggested that Mrs Simpson should go
abroad, he had seen it as an attempt to separate them; to
pay her off like a discarded mistress. But this fresh
suggestion was for her own safety. Her life was in danger
and no other consideration mattered.

'Very well, Chief Superintendent,' he said, 'I will see
what can be arranged.'

With Sinclair gone, the King went through to the
drawing-room where Wallis awaited him.

'How did you get on with Baldwin?' she asked. 'Did you
ask him about a wireless broadcast?'

'Later, Wallis darling. We have something more
important to discuss.' And he told her about the bomb
plot.

Her face paled. 'Why do people hate me so much that
they wish to kill me?'

The King took her in his arms. 'They don't know you as
I do, Wallis.'

She looked up at him with worried eyes. 'What are we
going to do, David?'

'Sinclair thinks the safest course is for you to go abroad.'

'And what do you think, David?'

The King hesitated a moment before saying, 'I agree
with Sinclair. Out of England you'll be safe.'

For perhaps the first time in her life Wallis Simpson was
truly frightened. Her liaison with the King, she now saw,
had stirred emotions so deep in the English spirit that
people were planning to kill her. 'I could go to Cannes,'
she said. 'Herman and Katherine will give me sanctuary.'

Herman and Katherine Rogers had been friends of hers
since those long-ago days in Peking when she had been
the wife of a mere naval lieutenant. 'I'll phone Katherine at
once,' she said.

There was no STD system of international telephoning in those days, but a cumbersome and sometimes time-consuming linkage through manual operators. So the telephone call that Wallis Simpson made from Fort Belvedere to *Lou Viei*, the Rogers' villa in Cannes, was routed through operators in London and Paris. The French press having been far less reticent about the King's romantic attachment to Wallis Simpson than the British press had been so far, the English-speaking operator who handled the call in Paris, alerted by a casual mention of Mrs Simpson's name, could not resist listening in.

'Of course we'd be delighted to have you to stay with us, Wallis. When do you plan to come?'

'David thinks it would be best if I leave here after dark. Catch the night-ferry from Newhaven. Tomorrow night he thinks. Then I'll motor down from Dieppe. I don't know how long it will take. I'll call you again en route.'

Later that evening the Parisienne operator told her lover what she had overheard on the telephone. Her lover, a young Frenchman with an eye to the main chance, saw a quick way to make a few extra francs by tipping off the Paris newspapers. By the following morning the editors of those newspapers were instructing reporters and photographers to proceed tout de suite to Dieppe.

That same morning also saw the London newspapers following the lead set by their provincial counterparts and breaking their long self-imposed silence, so that the Duke of York, arriving back in London by train from Edinburgh, was horrified to see through the clouds of steam which wreathed the platform a line of placards proclaiming THE KING'S MARRIAGE.

At Scotland Yard Detective Sergeant Thompson, as brisk-looking as ever despite only a few hours' sleep, was reporting the result of further inquiries made the previous evening in London and Kent. 'Hasn't been seen at either place since the Tuesday of last week,' he told Chief Superintendent Sinclair.

'You were discreet, I trust.'

'Discretion itself, sir. But I did pick up a bit of servants' gossip. One of the guns is missing from the gun-room.'

'That photo from the *Tatler* arrived yet?'

'Yes, sir. Copies are being run off now.'

'As soon as they're done get an artist to make a drawing from the photograph with spectacles and a lot more hair. Then get copies of that made too. Have both copies shown round the Cumberland Terrace area. Don't forget St Katherine's. And any public houses around there. And garages. May have hired a car. Or bought one. And have copies sent to Windsor to be shown around pubs and garages there.'

'Windsor, sir?'

'Yes, sergeant. And impress upon everyone involved to call in immediately if they turn up anything. Then inform me at once. If I'm not here, my secretary will know where I can be contacted.'

The Chief Superintendent now knew – or thought he knew – the identity of the sniper whose bullet had shattered the window of No.16. An arrest was simply a matter of time. The bomb-plotters, because their number and some of their identities were still unknown, posed a more serious threat. The sooner Mrs Simpson was out of the country, he thought, the better.

At Fort Belvedere the King was taking urgent steps to ensure the safety of the woman he loved. His own detective, Evans, must accompany her to Cannes, he decided. His own chauffeur, Ladbrook, would drive her. Good men, both of them. Reliable. Trustworthy. But it needed someone with them to make any urgent decisions that might be necessary. Monckton? No, he was needed here. Perry Brownlow? Just the man. A former Guards officer with a fine record, the 6th Baron Brownlow[3] held the normally undemanding royal post of Lord in Waiting.

The King reached for the telephone. 'Perry,' he said when he was connected. 'There's something I wish you to do for me.' The spirit of adventure came upon him. 'A special mission.' Before lunch time Perry Brownlow was at the Fort. The King explained the situation to him.

'Now here's the plan, Perry,' he went on. 'I want you to escort Wallis to Cannes. Evans will go with you for protection. Ladbrook my chauffeur, will drive you once you get to France. Book passages for the four of you on the night ferry to Dieppe. Use a nom-de-plume. Secrecy is vital. I don't want Wallis leaving here in her own car or mine. Someone would be bound to recognize it. What I propose is that Ladbrook collects her car from Cumberland Terrace, drives it to Newhaven and puts it aboard the ferry. Then tonight you come here again. No, make it late afternoon. There are pressmen hanging around the gate. They'll see you arrive and then when you leave again, after dark, they won't be suspicious. Wallis will be with you, of course, but she can crouch down between the seats until you're clear of the Fort.'

Wallis had listened to all this without interruption. Now she spoke. 'I'll need more clothes, David.'

'Of course, darling. But you mustn't go back to Cumberland Terrace. It isn't safe.'

'I know, David. I thought my maid, Burke, might go with Ladbrook when he collects the Buick. I can give her a list of what I need. She can pack them and Ladbrook can take them straight to Newhaven.'

Lord Brownlow took his leave, but returned in time for afternoon tea. By seven o'clock Mrs Simpson's luggage had been loaded into Brownlow's car. It was dark and drizzling with rain as the three of them – the King, Wallis and Brownlow – came out of the Fort. The King took Wallis in his arms.

'I shall never give you up,' he said.

He stood at the door, a sad, lonely figure, as the car pulled away, with Wallis, the woman who had hoped to be Queen, crouching like a stowaway between the seats so that no one outside might witness her departure.

Parting from Wallis, though it saddened the King, had also served to harden him. He was determined to have one more go at presenting his case to the people of Britain in the form of a wireless broadcast. Throughout the day, in between planning Mrs Simpson's flight to France and fussing round her, as he was wont to do, he had been working on a suitable script, writing and re-writing, re-phrasing and polishing. He had telephoned Baldwin at Downing Street and summoned him to another audience at Buckingham Palace that evening. Now he had one last glance through his intended broadcast before going out and climbing into his car for the drive to London.

But if the King was determined, he found Baldwin stubbornly obstinate.

For a time the two of them haggled politely back and forth, the King endeavouring to persuade – King though he was, he could not insist – and the Prime Minister immune to all persuasion.

'Sir, my advice is still that you should not broadcast,' Baldwin said presently, knowing that the King was constitutionally bound to act on his advice. 'For you to do so would serve only to harden public opinion. Indeed, it might serve to divide the country – split the nation.'

'I have a right to speak' the King persisted.

Baldwin did not reply.

'You want me to go, don't you?' the King said, petulantly.

'No, Sir,' Baldwin said again. 'I want you to stay. But to abandon this idea of marrying Mrs Simpson.'

'I have a right to marry; I have a right to happiness. I cannot be King without her. I will abdicate rather than give her up.'

'Sir,' said Baldwin, 'if that is your decision – if you must go – then go with dignity.'

While the King and his Prime Minister were haggling back and forth at Buckingham Palace, a short distance away, at Marlborough House, the Duke of York and his wife were dining with the Duke's mother, Queen Mary.

'I wish I knew more what was going on,' sighed the Duke. 'Will David give her up, do you think? If he doesn't it seems from the newspapers that there is only one other course.'

'Abdication,' said his mother, tight-lipped.

'Then I – we –' The Duke looked at his wife as though seeking support and reassurance. Both knew that if his brother abdicated, the Duke would be King. It was an honour neither of them sought or desired.

'He can't go,' said the Duke. 'The nation needs him. He's the right man for the job. He's been trained for it all his life. I have never even seen a state paper. I wouldn't know what to do.'

In saying which, as future history would show, he did himself a great deal less than justice.

'How is David?' he asked his mother.

'Don't ask me,' Queen Mary said, testily. 'I haven't seen hair or hide of him for the past ten days. But knowing you were coming to dinner, I sent him a message asking him to join us.'

It was late when the King arrived. He looked tense and strained. 'I have just had another session with Baldwin. He won't give an inch. It's all over, I fear.'

The Duke and Duchess looked at each other, their eyes conveying words their lips could not frame. Then the Duke said, 'I need to talk to you David.' He still had a forlorn hope that he might yet persuade the King to give up Wallis Simpson.

'Very well; come and see me tomorrow at the Fort. But I warn you – it will make no difference.'

The following day as was their custom when in London, the Duke and Duchess drove to Windsor to spend a weekend in the country with their two small daughters. From their country home, Royal Lodge, the Duke telephoned his brother at Fort Belvedere to ask when it would be convenient to drive over and talk to him.

To his astonishment, his brother's response was abrupt almost to the point of rudeness.

'Not today, Bertie. Call me again tomorrow.'

For the King, his brother's call had come at the wrong moment. He had more urgent matters on his mind. Since their meeting the previous evening events had taken a more dramatic – and potentially much more dangerous – turn.

The Journal
(December 3–4)

It was sheer luck that I glimpsed Mrs S as she left Fort Belvedere that Thursday evening. Paradoxically, had I been less bone-weary, so fatigued that I fell asleep while on watch, I would not have done so.

It was the first sight of her I had had since commencing my new vigil nearly seventy-two hours before. I had established a routine which I thought would afford me sufficient rest. Each morning, before dawn, I made my way over the wall, through the trees and took up position in the shrubbery which gave me a clear view of the front door. For three days, twelve hours a day, I had lain there, watching, waiting, subsisting on chocolate, lemonade and the occasional sip of cognac. There were times when I would have given anything for a cigarette, but smoking was out of question.

From my hiding-place I had a clear view of everyone who came and went – and there was a deal of coming and going. Twice I glimpsed the King as he walked outside to see someone off. The change in him was shocking. He was no longer dashing and boyish-looking. Now he looked his age, and more than his age, strained and worried. She had done that to him. Of her there was never a sign until that Thursday evening.

Each evening, as darkness fell, I retreated to where I had hidden the motor-bicycle, mounting it to ride into Windsor, where I left it in the lock-up garage while I went to get something to eat and replenish my supplies. The only eating place I could find open was a fish-and-chip shop. Each evening I bought myself what I discovered was known as 'a piece and a pennorth' – total cost threepence – which I carried away unhygenically wrapped in an old piece of newspaper and ate with my fingers.

I had also found a small back-street shop, run by a white-haired old lady, which remained open until late in the evening. There, each night, after consuming my fish and chips, I replenished my provisions, buying just sufficient to see me through the following day's vigil. Then it was back to my hide-out among the trees for a final cigarette before crawling into my sleeping-bag. Statistically, I should have had adequate sleep to see me through the next day, turning in about nine o'clock and rising between five and six in the morning, just sufficient time to have a breakfast of sorts before making my way to the shrubbery. In fact I had little sleep. The turmoil of my thoughts and the hardness of the ground combined to keep me awake for hours. Sleep itself was a succession of nightmares from which I would jerk awake, fearful of over-sleeping. I would switch on the flashlamp, screening it with my hand, to consult my watch only to find that it was no more than one o'clock, perhaps two or three, in the morning. That Thursday morning it had been three o'clock and I had lain awake for the rest of the night.

Concentration, in consequence, had been difficult. More than once I dozed off, only to snap awake again at the sound of a car coming or going. As on previous days, there had been a succession of visitors to the Fort. Most were strangers to me, but one I recognised – Lord Brownlow. I had met him in the past and knew him by sight. He came twice that day, arriving first in the morning and leaving again an hour or two later. Around four o'clock in the afternoon his Rolls-Royce purred up the drive again. It was shortly after that I fell asleep.

I was awakened by the sound of voices and a car engine starting up. It was dark and drizzling with rain, but not so dark that I could not see what was going on. Luggage was being loaded into a car. The car, in silhouette, was unmistakably a Rolls.

The front door of the Fort was open and an outside light on. Lord Brownlow appeared in the light followed by another man and a woman. The second man was the King. The chauffeur and another man climbed into the front of the Rolls. Lord Brownlow came round my side of the vehicle. The King and the woman embraced. I heard voices, but could not make out the words. But if the man was the King, then the woman had to be Mrs S.

The King helped her into the car. Lord Brownlow went back to speak to the King, then returned and climbed into the car also. The Rolls pulled away while the King stood waving.

Mrs S was leaving. The luggage which had been loaded suggested that she was not coming back, at least not for a few days. Probably she was returning to Cumberland Terrace. But I had to be sure.

I picked up the Mannlicher and slid it into the golf-bag. Then, golf-bag in one hand and haversack in the other, I retreated from the shrubbery, slid like a shadow across the narrow strip of grass and darted into the trees, scrambled over the wall and made for my motor-bicycle. It took me no more than a minute, maybe two, to locate my sleeping-bag, jam it into the haversack and fasten the haversack to the motor-cycle. I strapped the golf-bag across my back, pushed the motor-cycle on to the road, straddled it and operated the kick-start. The engine responded instantly.

I headed for the main gate. There was no sign of the Rolls. It must be somewhere ahead of me.

I might never have caught up with them – in which case I would have headed for Cumberland Terrace, which would have been totally wrong – but for another stroke of luck. Ahead of me, as I raced in pursuit, were the tail-lamps of a car parked at the side of the road. I was almost past it before I realised that it was a Rolls. The same Rolls? Surely it had to be though I couldn't for the life of me imagine why it should have stopped so soon.[1]

There was a gap in the hedgerow where a gate led into a field. I bumped across the grassy verge and pulled in beside it, cut the engine and switched off my lights. Mist was settling over the fields and the drizzling rain pitter-pattered on my leather gear. It seemed to me that I waited a long time; so long that I began to fear that I had made a mistake. Could it be that there was another Rolls in the vicinity that night? Two lovers parked by the roadside to do what lovers do in privacy.

I was about to kick-start the Norton again and head for Cumberland Terrace when headlamps came towards me; swept past. Unmistakably a Rolls, though misted windows and a darkened interior afforded no clue as to who was inside. I could only hope it was the right Rolls. I kicked the Norton into life and took up pursuit.

* * *

As the Rolls headed not for London but in a more or less south-easterly direction, I became more and more convinced that I was following the wrong car. But there seemed nothing for it now but to stick with it. If I was wrong, I could always head back for Cumberland Terrace. Following the Rolls south out of Lewes, I was on familiar ground. I had travelled this way before and had a pretty good idea where we were heading. Newhaven and the cross-channel ferry to Dieppe.

I followed them to the passenger terminal where Mrs S and Lord Brownlow got out. So did a second man. He gave no help with unloading the luggage. Not a servant then. Some sort of bodyguard perhaps. The chauffeur and a porter unloaded the luggage and followed Mrs S into the terminal building.

There seemed little doubt that she was leaving the country. But why? From the lingering manner in which she and the King had embraced it hardly seemed that they were parting for ever. Abdication. That was it. She was leaving. The King planned to abdicate and join her. But if she was dead, there would be no one to join; no point in abdicating. My mission had suddenly become more important than ever. At all costs I had to stay with her until a suitable opportunity presented itself.

One problem seemed insurmountable. I had no passport with me. Another problem was the question of petrol. Heavens knew how far I might have to travel in France, if I actually got to France, and the Norton's tank now was by no means full.

I parked the motor-bicycle on its stand and entered the passenger building. 'What time does the next ferry leave?' I asked a porter.

'Ten o'clock sharp.' He pointed through a window. 'That's it there.'

I looked at my wristwatch. There was time enough. I went back to the motor-cycle, kick-started it into life and retraced my route until I found a garage still open. A gallon of petrol cost me one shilling and tenpence. On my way back to the ferry terminal I passed the Rolls Royce, presumably on its way back.

I waited in the shadows of the terminal buildings, the engine of the Norton ticking over. Somehow I had to bluff my way aboard the ferry. In the misty yellow glow of the dockside lights I saw two dock workers getting ready to heave the gangplank clear. Others were in position to cast off the mooring-lines. Now was the time. I opened the throttle, raced round the passenger building, straight past the customs shed and on to the quayside, bringing the Norton to a halt at the foot of the gang-plank.

'Hold it a moment,' I said to the men on the gang-plank in my most authoritative voice. 'I have a message from His Majesty.' Then, dismounting, I ran up the gang-plank.

A ship's officer intercepted me at the top. I maintained the initiative. 'Where can I find Mrs Simpson?' I demanded.

He consulted a clipboard he was holding. 'There is no Mrs Simpson listed here,' he said.[2]

I judged him to be bluffing and continued with my own bluff. 'Conduct me to her at once. I have an urgent message from the King.'

'I think you'd better see the Captain,' the officer said.

'Certainly,' I snapped. 'Where do I find him?'

'On the bridge.'

He pointed. 'That companionway there. Then go forrad.'

'Thank you.' I turned away; turned back. 'While I'm seeing the Captain, have my motor-cycle brought aboard. I'm to go with Mrs Simpson.'

'I don't think –'

I cut his protest short. 'Those are the King's orders,' I said and walked quickly away. I climbed the companionway the officer had indicated. But I did not go 'forrad.' Instead, I went towards the stern of the ferry. Hidden in shadow, I waited to see if my bluff had worked. Orders were shouted, a davit slung out and a net lowered. The Norton was enmeshed in the net and slung aboard. Within minutes the ferry had sailed.

I saw nothing of either Mrs S or Lord Brownlow during the sea crossing. It was around midnight when the ferry docked at Dieppe. I mingled with other disembarking passengers and gained the quayside. There was nothing I could do about the Norton except hope that it would be put ashore. It was. Also off-loaded was a large and elegant car, a Buick. A uniformed chauffeur fussed around, making sure that no damage was done to the vehicle as the off-loading tackle was removed. Then I saw Lord Brownlow and Mrs S. They climbed into the rear of the Buick and it motored slowly towards the waiting customs officials. I collected the Norton and followed. Somehow – goodness knew how – I had to get past the customs barrier myself. Without a passport, it wasn't going to be easy.

The chauffeur climbed out of the Buick to attend to the customs formalities. Lord Brownlow followed. There apeared to be some difficulty. I was close enough to overhear one of the French customs officers say, 'Mais ce n'est pas Madame Harris. C'est Madame Simpson.'

It did not require a genius to work out what the problem was. For whatever reason Mrs S was travelling under an assumed name. But the passport was in her real name.[3]

Then I noticed something else – a small group of men with cameras massed just beyond the customs barrier. Photographers. Someone had alerted the French press.

The argument between Lord Brownlow and the customs officers continued. There seemed to be some insistence on the part of the customs men that Mrs S should get out of the car. She did so, closely followed by the man who seemed to be her bodyguard.

It was a heaven-sent opportunity.

'Voilà la dame,' I cried in my best French.

As I had hoped, complete confusion followed. The photographers rushed forward. The bodyguard tried to hold them back. Camera bulbs flashed. Lord Brownlow bundled Mrs S back into the Buick. The chauffeur climbed into the driving-seat. One of the customs men had been knocked down by the rush of photographers. Lord Brownlow was shouting through an open rear window … and the second customs man obligingly raised the barrier.

I kick-started the Norton into life. The Buick shot through the barrier – and so did I.

I tailed the Buick to Rouen where William the Conqueror died and Joan of Arc was burned at the stake. It halted outside the Hotel de la Poste. From some thirty or forty yards back, the engine of the Norton switched off and its lights extinguished, I watched Mrs S and Lord Brownlow enter the hotel. The chauffeur and the other man followed a few minutes later. It looked as though they were stopping there for what was left of the night.

I allowed them some twenty minutes to get settled, then went into the hotel myself. There was a night-porter on duty and I asked for a room. He pushed the register towards me. I signed in the name of Davis.

I have no recollection of what my room was like except that it contained a vast wardrobe with mirrored doors. Not that I used the wardrobe. I felt far too exhausted even to undress. I simply unstrapped the golf-bag, stood it in a corner near the bed, lay down and promptly fell fast asleep with the light still on.

Sounds of commotion awakened me. It was broad daylight. I climbed off the bed, crossed to the window and looked down into the street. The Buick was still there, people milling excitedly around it. I saw several cameras. The photographers from Dieppe had caught up, it seemed.

From my vantage point I saw the chauffeur get into the driving-seat. The bodyguard had the nearside rear door open. Lord Brownlow was trying to fight his way through the crowd, followed by Mrs Simpson. One of the photographers, a girl, was between Mrs S and the Buick, camera poised. The bodyguard lunged in her direction and the camera was sent flying.[4] Lord Brownlow helped Mrs S into the car.

Another minute and they would be on their way. I had no time to lose. I grabbed the golf-bag, strapping it on as I raced along the landing and down the stairs.

A female receptionist who was now on duty let out an excited shout in French as I ran towards the door. The doorman barred my way. It was frustrating to be waved back to the reception desk to settle my account. I had no French money and the minutes ticked agonisingly away as francs were laboriously translated into pounds sterling.

By the time I was out of the hotel there was no sign of the Buick. I took the N14 out of Rouen, judging that Mrs S was making for Paris. I rode flat out, hoping to overtake the Buick, but after forty kilometres, which I covered in well under that number of minutes, there was still no sign of it. I knew this part of France well from touring holidays since childhood and decided to cut across and try the N13. This brought me in due course to Evreux with its splendid Roman remains. But still no sign of the Buick.

It was close to lunch time and I was ravenous. It was days since I had had a proper meal and I had eaten nothing at all for quite eighteen hours. So I cruised slowly through Evreux in search of a suitable restaurant. My attention was caught by a crowd of people outside the Hotel du Grand Cerf. Beyond them a man stood in the hotel doorway. I recognised him instantly as the one who had knocked the camera from the girl photographer's hand in Rouen. More people were gathered round the entrance to the hotel courtyard. I brought the Norton to a standstill. Parked in the courtyard was the Buick.

11

Words of Warning
(December 4)

Britain, that first Friday in December, 1936, came as close to civil war as at any time since the seventeenth century. Baldwin had been right when he told the King that a wireless broadcast might divide the nation. Newspaper headlines had already wrought deep division. The ordinary people of London massed in front of Buckingham Palace with banners bearing the legend *God Save The King*. Members of Sir Oswald Mosley's so-called British Union of Fascists marched up and down Whitehall, chanting, 'Out with Baldwin. Death to Baldwin. Hang Baldwin.' Troopers at a cavalry barracks saddled their horses and belted on their side-arms ready to ride to the King's aid if called upon.

None of which concerned Chief Superintendent Sinclair. His sole concern was the King's safety. His worries were eased when he received word from the Special Branch that the muttered threats of the Empire Royalists were more wind than substance. Their bomb plot existed only in their own imaginations. They might wish to blast Wallis Simpson, the twice-divorced American, to Kingdom Come, but they had neither an actual bomb nor the technical know-how to construct one. However, his peace of mind was to be short-lived. It ended with the arrival in his office of Detective Sergeant Thompson.

'Just had word from Windsor,' Thompson told him.

'Someone there has identified the picture of the suspect. Chap who owns a garage. Recognised the suspect as soon as one of the local men showed him the photograph. Bought a motor-bike from him on Monday, he says, a Norton, and rented a lock-up garage to keep it in.'

'Is the motor-cycle in the garage?'

'No, sir. The place was locked. The owner gave our men permission to knock off the padlock. No motor-bike.'

'Did we get a description of what the suspect was wearing?'

'Yes, sir. Black leather motor-cycling gear with a helmet.'

'Bound to have goggles too for riding a motor-cycle. Good as a disguise that lot. Got the registration number?'

'Yes, sir.'Thompson read it out from a notebook he was holding and Sinclair jotted it down.

'All right, sergeant,' he said. 'Leave it with me.'

His mind, as the door closed behind Sergeant Thompson, was already running over the salient facts. Windsor was only a few miles from Fort Belvedere. No distance at all to someone on a motor-cycle. The suspect must know that Mrs Simpson was at the Fort; must be somewhere in that vicinity. He reached for his candlestick telephone.

'Please connect me with Inspector Evans at Fort Belvedere.'

But Inspector Evans, he was told when he was put through, was not there.

'Where is he?' he asked.

'I don't rightly know, sir,' the Fort Belvedere operator told him. 'I think he left last night.'

'Left? For where?'

'I don't know, sir. I think you should speak to the King, sir.'

There was a delay of nearly five minutes before he was put through. 'Yes, what is it, Sinclair?' the King demanded.

'Sir, I need to speak to Inspector Evans urgently. I understand that he is no longer at Fort Belvedere and that only you, Sir, know his whereabouts.'

'He's on a special job for me,' said the King. 'Look, we can't talk over the telephone. You'd better come here, Sinclair. Post haste.'

The King broke the connection. Puzzled, more worried than ever, Sinclair jiggled the receiver rest until the Scotland Yard operator came back on the line, then asked for his car to be brought round. Two more jiggles brought Sergeant Thompson and Sergeant Blunt to his office.

He told Thompson, 'Keep in close touch with the hunt for the suspect. Alert the Windsor area to watch out for that motor-cycle. If it's spotted, detain the rider. Keep me fully informed if anything materializes. I want to know at once – at once, you understand. You can get me at Fort Belvedere. I should be there in about forty-five minutes.' To Blunt he said, 'You come with me, sergeant.'

Arriving at the King's country house, he instructed Blunt to remain in the car. 'I'll send word out if I want you, sergeant.' Then he announced himself at the front door and was ushered into the King's presence.

The King waved him to a seat. 'Now what is it you want to see Evans about so urgently?'

Sinclair told him all that had transpired, right up to the purhase of a motor-cycle.

'You know who this person is?' the King asked.

'We think so, Sir. I've arranged for police in the Windsor area to watch out for and detain the suspect. Now if you will tell me where I can locate Inspector Evans, Sir. He needs to be put in the picture.'

The King gave his familiar quizzical smile. 'Inspector Evans is in France, Chief Superintendent.'

'In France!'

The King brought out his cigarette case, selected a cigarette, lit it. 'Let me put *you* in the picture, Chief Superintendent. Mrs Simpson left for France last night. On my instructions, Inspector Evans went with her. So, at my request, did Lord Brownlow. So we hardly need to worry about your motor-cyclist, I think.'

'With respect, Sir, she may have been followed.'

'Ah, but she did not use her own car. She travelled in Lord Brownlow's. At least to Newhaven. Her own car was taken there earlier in secret. And her passage was booked in a false name. Safe enough, don't you think?'

'One would think so, Sir,' Sinclair said, doubtfully. He still felt uneasy. 'Have you had word since her arrival in France?'

'Not yet, Chief Superintendent. She was going to call when they docked in Dieppe, but I imagine she didn't have time.'

The telephone rang at that moment. A relieved smile illuminated the King's face, 'That could be Mrs Simpson.'

Sinclair started to get up with the intention of withdrawing. But the King gestured to him to remain seated. 'I may need you.' he picked up the telephone.

'What? I can't hear you … Is that you, Wallis? … This is a deuced bad connection … You're where? … Evreux? … That's not on your route … What in the world are you doing there? … You're being followed?'

Sinclair, who had been staring fixedly at the carpet, trying to pretend he was not listening, looked up, startled.

'Photographers,' said the King into the telephone. 'How the devil did they find out?'

He seemed irritated, but otherwise unconcerned. Not so the Chief Superintendent. If the newspapers had found out about Mrs Simpson's flight from Britain, then so perhaps had someone else.

There followed a long silence on the King's part as he listened to his beloved Wallis, almost shouting to make herself heard, imperiously informing him that he must on no account 'stand down'. The King, reaching over to stub out his cigarette, noticed Sinclair signalling to him with a flicking forefinger.

'If I could have a word with Inspector Evans, Sir,' the Chief Inspector murmured.

The King put his hand momentarily over the mouthpiece. 'I'd prefer you spoke to Lord Brownlow.'

Sinclair nodded assent. The King shouted into the telephone, 'Listen to me a moment, Wallis, please. Is Perry with you? Put him on, will you?' He gestured to Sinclair to take over the telephone.

'This is Chief Superintendent Sinclair, your lordship.'

'I can't hear you. Who did you say?'

Sinclair repeated his name. Almost shouting to make himself heard, so bad was the connection, obliged to repeat nearly everything twice and sometimes three times, he explained the situation to Lord Brownlow. Mrs Simpson, now that she was in France, was unlikely to be in danger, but he could not afford to take the chance. He had to repeat the registration number of the motor-cycle several times before Lord Brownlow said, 'Got it.'

'Finished?' the King asked. Sinclair nodded. 'Then give me the telephone.'

Sinclair passed it over. 'Perry,' the King shouted, 'this is the King. You'd better alert Evans and Ladbrook. But don't tell Wallis. I don't want her worried. I know I can rely on you to take good care of her.' There was a pause, then the King said, 'Now put her back on the line, please.'

Sinclair strolled to the window, looking out, trying to close his ears to the King's shouted endearments. 'Call me again when you can, Wallis dearest. Wherever you stop tonight. You can't possibly get there today now. Take care, my darling.'

It was with obvious reluctance that he finally replaced the telephone. Scarcely had he done so than it rang again. Frowning, the King picked it up with an impatient gesture. The caller this time, though Sinclair could not know this, was the King's brother, the Duke of York. 'Not today, Bertie,' Sinclair heard the King say. 'Call me again tomorrow.'[1]

'With your permission, Sir, I think I should inform the Sureté,' Sinclair said as the King replaced the telephone. 'Have them assign men to protect the lady.'

'Good lord, no,' the King exclaimed. 'You know what the French are. It will be all over the newspapers in no time.'

However, he did agree that another Yard man, trained in the use of firearms, should serve as his own bodyguard until the return of Inspector Evans, and Sinclair drove back to London satisfied that he had done all he could to safeguard the King. And that was his principal concern.

With any luck the motor-cyclist suspect would soon be pulled in. Though he had deemed it advisable to warn Lord Brownlow, he did not really think that the would-be assassin could have crossed the Channel.

Nor, when he thought about it logically, did the King. All the same he was desperately worried. His mind dwelt constantly on his beloved Wallis. Winston Churchill, arriving at the Fort that evening, found him almost apathetic towards the growing constitutional crisis. Churchill did his best to rally him – 'You must fight, Sir. You owe it to yourself and the country' – but was driven more and more to the conviction that he was talking to a monarch who no longer cared whether he remained on the throne or not.

The King's concern – now – was only for Wallis. As the day passed with no further word from her, logic gave way to fantasy. To be parted from her was bad enough. The thought of possible danger to her was torment. He must hope that Perry and Evans, between them, would keep her safe.

Across the Channel, in Evreux, like the fine officer he was, Lord Brownlow had already disposed the slender forces under his present command to best advantage. On the gentlemanly pretext of 'washing my hands', he excused himself from Mrs Simpson's side to seek out Inspector Evans and Ladbrook and alert them to the situation. He stressed to them, as the King had stressed to him, that Mrs Simpson was not to be worried. He passed on to them the registration number of the motor-cycle and despatched them to check the environs of the hotel.

He was lunching with Mrs Simpson when Inspector Evans spotted the motor-cycle parked in the hotel courtyard.

12

The Journal
(December 4)

I turned into the hotel courtyard and cruised slowly past the Buick. There was no one in it or anywhere near it. I parked the Norton near a range of stables at the far end of the courtyard and tried the nearest door. It was locked. So was the next one. But the third opened for me and I slipped inside.

The interior had a low, beamed ceiling and a cobbled floor with a gulley running down the middle. But these days it was apparently used as a storehouse rather than a stable, with iron-hooped barrels and wooden packing-cases stacked along two sides. The door opened outwards. It had originally been in two halves, but at some time in the past the halves had been joined by a couple of vertical battens. There was a small cobwebbed window high in the rear wall. I closed the door to leave an aperture of about six inches, knelt on the cobbles, eased the Mannlicher from the golf-bag and sighted along it. Most of the Buick was in my field of fire and I had every chance of making a clean kill.

But making a getaway would not be so easy. The best thing would be to move the Norton inside with me, kick it into life the moment I had shot Mrs S, then race across the courtyard while those with her were still shocked and confused.

I was about to put this part of my plan into operation when I spotted the man I took to be her bodyguard. He was walking towards the Buick. He paused briefly and appeared to be examining the interior of the Buick through its windows. Then he looked round, seemed to stiffen and moved towards where I had parked the Norton. Gently, silently, I eased the stable door shut.

The rusty bolt made a small grating sound as I slid it into its socket. My mouth felt dry and I could feel myself perspiring.

I strained my ears to catch the sound of his footsteps. They stopped for a moment, then started again.

'Sacré bleu.'

The exclamation came from behind me; from the other end of the stable. I whipped round to see a man standing in another doorway at the far end. I pointed the rifle at him. It was not yet loaded, but he could not know that.

'Entrez' *I said.*

He shuffled clear of the doorway.

'Fermez la porte.'

Obediently he closed the door behind him.

'Silence,' *I ordered him.*

He was short and squat, with wide, powerful shoulders. There was a dirty apron fastened round his waist and above it he wore a faded blue shirt. Despite the coldness of the day, the shirtsleeves were rolled up to reveal muscular arms covered in a mass of black hairs.

'Ici,' *I said, jerking my head. He shuffled forward a few paces. I stood up and moved round, keeping my distance. I did not want those big hands of his making a grab at the rifle.*

Outside in the courtyard, the footsteps came closer. Now they were right outside where I was hiding. The bolt rattled in its socket as the man tried the door. A pause. The footsteps moved on. I realised that I had been holding my breath. The footsteps receded into the distance.

I now had the problem of what to do about the man who had surprised me. A coil of wire hung from a rusty nail, but to tie him would mean putting down the rifle and I didn't fancy the idea of venturing within reach of those powerful hands. A large cask stood among the boxes and barrels. Keeping the rifle trained on him with one hand, I moved over to it and lifted the lid. It was nearly half full of what smelled like sour wine. I put the lid down beside the barrel and gestured with the rifle.

'Get in,' *I said in French.*

I backed away, the rifle still pointed at him, as he moved over to the barrel. He looked inside it, looked at me, shook his head.

'In,' *I said, making my voice as menacing as possible.*

He pulled one of the boxes over, stood on it and climbed

awkwardly into the barrel. He stood there looking at me.

'Get down.'

His ape-like face registered fury, but he did as I said. The contents of the barrel, displaced by his body, came up to his shoulders. I clapped the lid back in place. Now that he could no longer see me, I put down the rifle and picked up the box on which he had stood. It was heavier than I had thought – he had lifted it with apparent ease – but I managed to heft it on top of the barrel. I lifted another box on top of the first. Even that combined weight, I felt, would not resist those powerful shoulders for long once he tried to get out.

There were voices outside; a car engine came to life. I drew back the bolt and eased open the stable door fractionally … just in time to see the Buick pulling out of the courtyard.

I returned the Mannlicher to the golf-bag, dashed to the Norton, gave it a kick-start and set off in pursuit. There was no sign of the Buick when I reached the entrance to the courtyard. I rode to the town centre and paused there to study the direction signs. They would surely have followed the N14 from Rouen if Paris was their destination. By the same token, they would surely have taken a different route from Rouen if Mrs S was intending to hide out at Dinard, Deauville, Trouville or somewhere else along the coast. Or if she was making for Cherbourg or Brest to board a liner for her native America. So, by a process of elimination, I deduced that the Buick was heading south. I decided to try the N154.

By mid-afternoon I was in Chartres. It has several hotels, but only two, I thought, of a standard to satisfy Mrs S – La France and the Grand Monarque. They were conveniently located together in the Place des Epars, but there was no sign of the Buick at either. I was disappointed, but not surprised. Assuming they had lunched at Evreux, there was no reason to stop again in Chartres. Orleans lay seventy-odd kilometres further on, a convenient place to spend the night. Darkness was falling and the weather was noticeably colder as I headed south.

13

The King's Decision
(December 4)

In her memoirs the Duchess of Windsor states that, leaving Evreux, they 'somehow took the wrong road.' More probably, even if she was unaware of the fact, the diversion was deliberate, designed either to check whether they were still being followed or to confuse anyone who was following them. Either way, it meant that it was after dark before they reached Orleans, the city from which Joan of Arc had embarked upon her ill-fated crusade to rid France of the English five centuries before.

They parked out of sight up a side street, with Lord Brownlow and Inspector Evans keeping watch while Wallis Simpson spent an hour trying to get through to the King by telephone. She was unsuccessful. By that time it had begun to snow, and by the time they reached Blois, sixty kilometres further on in the valley of the Loire, further progress was clearly impossible and it was decided to spend the night at the Hotel de France et de Guise. From there she tried again to telephone the King and this time she was successful.[1]

The King had dined that evening with a handful of his most loyal supporters, among them Winston Churchill and Walter Monckton. Throughout the meal Churchill continued to urge that the King must 'stand and fight'. Walter Monckton, living at the Fort, acting as the King's go-between with the Government, must surely have sensed that the King had little stomach for further fight.

The others had left, Monckton had withdrawn to go through some papers and only Churchill remained, puffing on a cigar, when a footman entered to say that the King was wanted on the telephone. The King's face, drawn and strained throughout dinner, came suddenly alive. He almost bounded through to the library.

'That you, Wallis?' he shouted into the telephone. 'How are you? Are you at Cannes?'

'No,' she told him. 'At Blois. At the Hotel de France et de Guise. We had to stop here because of the weather. It's snowing like anything.'

'But you're all right, Wallis?'

'Hold on a moment, David. Perry's just come in.' The King heard her say, 'What is it, Perry?' but failed to hear Lord Brownlow's reply. Then Wallis spoke again.

'It seems the newspapers have caught up with us. Perry says the hotel lobby is packed with reporters and photographers. More than twenty of them.'

'Any sign –'

The King stopped abruptly. He had been about to ask if there was any sign of the motor-cyclist, but had no wish to alarm Wallis. Instead, he said, 'Let me have a word with Perry, will you?'

'Sorry, David – he's gone again. Said something about wanting to see Inspector Evans.'

'Then get him back, Wallis.'

It was concern for her which brought a flash of anger to the King's voice. But she could not be expected to know that. 'Really, David,' she reprimanded him in school-marmish fashion.

'I'm sorry, darling,' the King apologised, 'but it is most important that I –'

At that moment there was a click and the line went dead. Frantically the King jiggled the ear-piece rest until the Fort Belvedere operator came on the line.

'I've been cut off,' the King told him abruptly. 'Have me re-connected.'

'Where to, Your Majesty?'

'France – Blois – the Hotel de France and something,' the King said, impatiently, then slammed down the ear-piece.

For nearly an hour, while Churchill, in the dining-room, wondered what was keeping the King, the operator sought to re-establish contact with the hotel in Blois. In the library the King paced restlessly back and forth, chain-smoking cigarette after cigarette. More than once, increasingly worried, he picked up the telephone to ask the operator how things were going. The answer was always the same: 'I'm still trying, Your Majesty.'

The King's distraught mind conjured up fantastic and unnerving images. Wallis being brutally murdered as she lay in her bed. He must do something. He must be at her side. He rang for his footman. 'I need a map of France.' Then he walked back to where Churchill sat alone in the dining-room.

'I have to go to France,' he said.

Churchill took what remained of his cigar from his mouth. 'May I ask why, Sir?'

'Because the woman I love is in danger.' Briefly, succinctly, he told Churchill what had transpired.

'If I may venture a suggestion, Sir, would it not be better to ask Scotland Yard to send more men over?'

'No, I must go myself. I must be with her. It is on my account that she is in danger.'

'You may be putting yourself in danger, Sir.'

The King gave a bleak smile. 'You're a fine one to talk about putting yourself in danger, Winnie. You have done so many times.'

'But I am not the King, Sir.'

The footman came into the room. 'A map of France, Your Majesty.'

The King opened the map, pushed his wine glass and fruit plate aside, and spread it on the table. 'They're spending the night at Blois. Where the deuce is that? Ah, here it is.'

'How do you propose to travel to France, Sir?' Churchill inquired.

'Fly, of course,' said the King. 'If I fly out tonight perhaps I can catch up with them before they leave Blois in the morning.'

'You can't possibly fly tonight, Sir,' Churchill said. 'Not

in this weather.'

'Then first thing in the morning. I'll telephone Croydon and tell them to have my aeroplane ready at first light. I'll make for Lyon and hope to intercept them there.'

Churchill stubbed out his cigar, pushed back his chair and came to his feet. 'If you are determined to go, Sir, then I shall come with you.'

The King looked at him doubtfully, trying to remember how old Churchill was. Had to be in his early sixties. Too old for the sort of hazards that might lie ahead.

'I appreciate the offer, Winnie, but it will be better if you remain here. My brother will be wanting to see me. Baldwin will doubtless be in touch. I rely upon you to deal with them discreetly.'

But the man who, in his younger days, had fought in Cuba, India, Egypt and South Africa, who had been captured by the Boers and escaped within a month, who had commanded the 6th Royal Scots Fusiliers in Belgium during the Great War, was not to be deterred as easily as that. The scent of adventure was again in his nostrils.

'With respect, Sir,' he said, 'Walter Monckton can deal with them better than I could.'

The Journal
(December 4–5)

Arriving in Orleans, I headed straight for the town's leading hotel in the Quai Cypierre. The street was crammed with cars, many badly parked, and across from the hotel entrance were rival newsreel vans, cameramen with tripod-mounted cameras perched precariously on top. Others had already caught up with Mrs S, it seemed.

I parked the Norton and headed towards the mob of photographers and journalists gathered in front of the hotel. Even as I did so, two men rushed out of the hotel, shouting and gesticulating excitedly. They spoke in French, but I got the gist.

'You American?' asked a voice with an American accent.

'No – English,' I said.

'You parley the lingo; understand what they're on about?'

I nodded. 'She's not booked in here.'

'Then where the hell is she? She was sure headed this way.' He scratched his chin. 'What paper you with?'

'Morning Post,' *I lied.*

'Daily Record,' *said the American.* 'New York.'

Another car pulled up with a screech of brakes and two more men jumped out, shouting in French.

'What are those guys on about?' asked my new-found acquaintance.

'They've just checked the Hotel Martroi and the Moderne,' I translated for him. 'She's not at either of those.'

The French contingent jabbered excitedly among themselves. Then one dashed back into the hotel.

'What gives?' asked the American.

'He's going to call La République,' I said. 'It's the local newspaper. They're hoping someone there may know something.'

'Praise heaven for someone who knows the lingo,' said the American. 'Jesus, if it ain't snowing.'

Suddenly the hotel door jerked open again and the French newsman came hurrying out, shouting as he came. The group on the pavement split up, running towards different cars.

'What now?' asked the American.

'Mrs Simpson was here about an hour ago,' I said. 'Her car took the road to Blois.'

'Let's get going then. You want a hitch?'

'No, thanks,' I said. 'I've got my own transport.'

By then the first press car was already on its way. The others followed, a noisy cavalcade of revving engines and shouted voices. I returned to the Norton, kicked it into life and tagged on behind.

Blois was some sixty kilometres. For me, with snow falling, it was an uncomfortable ride. I was frequently compelled to steer with one hand while I used the other to clear my goggles. I was puzzled about Blois. Bourges would surely have been a more direct route to the Riviera. But Mrs S and her party were there all right, the now familiar Buick parked outside the Hotel de France.

The press contingent screeched to a halt and the whole mob stamped into the hotel, besieging the concierge, commandeering chairs and sofas, ordering drinks, coffee, sandwiches. I followed them in, brushing snow from my leathers.

My American friend spotted me and came over. 'What's with the golf-bag?' he asked.

'Disguise,' I said. 'So I don't look like a reporter.'

He grinned. 'You figure that helps?'

At the far end of the lobby I glimpsed a familiar face, Lord Brownlow. He surveyed the milling mob of reporters, photographers and newsreel men with a look of consternation. Then he withdrew as quickly as he had come.

I ordered myself a café au lait and some sandwiches, then realised that I had no French money with which to pay. 'Is English money all right?' I asked the waiter who attended to me, proffering a five-pound note.

'Oui,' he said, nodding. My change, when it came, was in francs.

Gradually the mob of pressmen settled down, talk giving way to the chewing of sandwiches and the slurping of drink. Two of the French contingent settled themselves at a table with a pack of cards. The American stretched himself out on a sofa. 'Wake me if anything gives,' he said, and closed his eyes.

It was about an hour later when the bodyguard came into the lobby. He went over to the concierge and asked about telephoning. The concierge nodded and pointed. There was a public telephone fixed to the wall of the lobby, but I couldn't imagine he was going to make a call in the hearing of so many pressmen.

Nor did he. As he stood there, as though making up his mind, Lord Brownlow came back into the lobby.

'Ah, there you are, Evans,' he said. So that was his name, Evans. The stretched-out American opened his eyes and the rest of the press party became similarly alert. 'Just want to let you know that we'll be leaving at nine o'clock in the morning.'

'So now we know,' murmured the American. 'Good night, all.' And he closed his eyes again.

Lord Brownlow withdrew from the lobby and a minute or so later Evans followed him. Though he had inquired about a telephone, he had made no attempt to use it. Was that because some at least of the pressmen would have overheard every word he said? Or was it because he had never had any intention of using it? Had it been a pretext for him to be in the lobby as one of the players in a pretty piece of play-acting? Lord Brownlow was not a fool. Unless he wanted the press for company, which seemed highly unlikely, he would not have announced their intended time of departure for all the world to hear.

The more I thought about it, the more convinced I was that his lordship was up to something. The announcement of a nine-o'clock departure was a trick. They intended to sneak away much earlier. But how? They could hardly slip out through the lobby, crowded as it was with reporters and photographers.

On the pretext of looking for the toilets, I picked my way through the outstretched legs of the eating, drinking, lolling, catnapping pressmen and investigated the domestic quarters of the hotel. Room-service waiters were hardly likely to use the main stairs. There had to be another route to the guest bedrooms. There was. Beyond the hotel kitchen were the back stairs. Down the back stairs, through the kitchen, then round to where the Buick was *parked – that was the way they would leave.*

The rear door of the kitchen was locked, but the key was in the lock. I turned it and went outside. The snow was turning to a wetting sleet. I made my way round to the front of the hotel. Two of the press mob, I saw, had parked their cars strategically close to the Buick. Expert though the chauffeur must be, he was going to have difficulty extricating himself without banging into one or other. Further along the street, I found the Norton was now similarly jammed between a couple of cars. I manoeuvred it clear, wheeled it further along the street and parked it afresh. It might be required in a hurry.

I went back into the hotel through the kitchen and mounted the back stairs. This brought me to a small passage on the upper floor. Beyond the passage carpeted corridors with doors spaced along them joined at right angles. Continuing on, hoping for some clue as to which was Wallis Simpson's room, I found myself on a gallery leading to the main staircase. The voices of the reporters staked out in the hotel lobby were plainly audible. Another corridor at the far end of the gallery led me to the rear of the building and so back to where I had started. It was then that I spotted a door in the passage leading to the back stairs. Unlike the guest bedrooms, it had no number and was fitted with a snick-catch instead of a door-knob. Opening it revealed a walk-in linen closet. I slipped inside, closing the door behind me as far as was possible without engaging the snick-catch.

Lighting in the upstairs corridors had been dimmed for the night, but opening the closet door a fraction more afforded sufficient illumination to see what I was about. I lifted down some spare bolsters to make a bed of sorts, put the golf-bag beside it with a blanket to conceal it, got another blanket for myself and lay on the bolsters to rest and think.

It would be too risky, I reasoned, to try and take Mrs S on the back stairs. My own escape could be too easily cut off. I needed to be downstairs ahead of her and take her as she emerged into the kitchen. Unlock the back door first and I could be straight out.

But I would have to watch out for the man called Evans. If he was there to act as bodyguard to Mrs S, as I suspected, he was probably armed, and almost certainly a crack shot.

If my guess was correct, they would be up and away while it was still dark.[1] I wondered what time the kitchen staff came on duty and *whether …*

I hadn't intended to sleep, but it had been a long day and my body and mind were alike exhausted. I had been frozen on the motor-cycle. Now, as my body-warmth built up again in my cocoon of bolsters and blankets, I felt totally relaxed, and I slept.

I was awakened by the sound of footsteps and the rattle of crockery. I didn't want to wake. I wanted to stay asleep. There was the sound of knocking. A voice said, 'Trois heures, M'sieur. Ici votre café.'

Almost fully awake now, I crawled round so that I could see through the crack between door and frame. The night porter (or so I took it to be) was halfway along the landing, balancing a loaded tray on one hand while he opened a door with the other. Then he disappeared inside the room.

It was my chance to reach the kitchen. I turned to pick up the Mannlicher. But before I could slip out of my hiding-place the porter was saying, 'Merci, m'sieur. Merci beaucoup,' and backing out of the room again.

He marched back along the corridor, jingling some coins in his hand. I drew back into the shadow of the closet. He could not have seen me, but must have spotted that the closet door was not properly closed. There was a small click as he went past and my small sliver of light vanished. Worse still, I was locked in. Explore as I would by sense of touch, I failed to locate any way of opening the door from inside the closet.

I pushed against the door. It yielded fractionally and I judged that the catch was a flimsy one held in place by a few screws. I was about to barge the door with my shoulder when I heard feet again ascending the back stairs. Someone went past the closet and there was the sound of voices, though they were too far off for me to make out the words.

Feet came back along the corridor. From further off a voice called out, 'Tell Ladbrook I'll be right down. We'll see if we can push it out of the way.'

The feet retreated down the back stairs. I waited a moment more before barging my way out. It was as well that I did so. There were more voices – coming nearer. A man and a woman. The woman's voice said something about 'something to eat'.

'We'll be in Moulins in time for breakfast,' the man replied in a cultured voice that could belong only to Lord Brownlow.

At least I knew where they were heading. I heard them start down the back stairs.

Now!

I barged the door with my shoulder. The catch splintered from the woodwork and I was free. Golf-bag in hand, I crept down the stairs and peered through the glass panel of the swing door into the kitchen. I was just in time to see the night porter follow them out, closing the outside door behind him. I glanced at my watch. It was half past three.

I crossed the kitchen and went out through the back door. It was still sleeting. Cautiously, I made my way to the front of the hotel. Shadowy figures moved around the parked cars; voices spoke in whispers. I heard a voice say, 'Start up and see if you can push them out of the way.'

As I had anticipated, they were having trouble extricating the Buick from the press cars parked fore and aft. Car doors opened and clicked shut. The Buick's engine came smoothly to life. At any moment I expected journalists to come pelting out of the hotel. But they remained where they were, seemingly unaware that their quarry was getting away.

I could just make out the movements of the Buick as it shunted the other cars clear until finally sufficient space had been created for it to pull away. And still the alarm had not been raised. It sped away into the darkness, its tail-lights almost immediately obscured by the wind-blown sleet. The night porter was still around somewhere. I remained hidden until I heard him walk away up the side passage. There was no necessity for me to sit on the Buick's tail. I knew they planned to breakfast in Moulins. I walked to where the Norton was parked, strapped on the golf-bag, kicked the engine into life and took up the hunt.

Those two hundred kilometres between Blois and Moulins were a nightmare. The sleet again fogged my goggles until I could hardly see and several times I had to steer with one hand while I wiped them clear with the other. Once, while I was doing this, the motor-cycle slid pefrom usly sideways on the slippery road surface and I only just avoided coming a cropper. After that I reduced speed so that I travelled within range of the uncertain yellow beam cast by my headlamp. To add to my troubles, I ran out of petrol and found myself pushing the Norton a kilometre or more to reach Villeneuve-sur-Allier. The garage there was not yet open for the day and I had to pound on the door to bring a grumbling proprietor downstairs. He was not at all happy about my English banknotes, but the timely production of a gold sovereign changed his tune, though he took a bite at it with stained and broken teeth before finally accepting it.

The result of all this was that I nearly missed Mrs S in Moulins. Breakfast over, they were already setting off again when I caught up with them. I followed at a discreet distance as they headed in the direction of Lyon.

Royal Pursuit
(December 5)

It was not yet dawn when the royal Daimler, the King himself at the wheel, arrived at the Aerodrome, Croydon. The two controllers on duty in the tower looked up in startled surprise as he walked in followed by Winston Churchill.

'Please sit down,' the King said as they came quickly to their feet. 'No formality. I'm flying to Sandringham. How soon can you clear me for take-off?'

'Not until daylight at least, Your Majesty,' said the senior of the controllers, 'and perhaps not then unless the weather clears. It's pretty murky at present.'

'Damn the weather,' said the King. 'I need to be away at first light.' He turned abruptly on his heel and walked out.

The King led the way across the airfield to the hangar which housed the two Dragon Rapides of The King's Flight. Formation of the Flight had been one of the first actions of the new reign.

A sergeant mechanic and two aircraftmen of the Royal Air Force were busy servicing one of the Rapides. 'Ten-shun,' the sergeant barked as the King entered the hangar.

'Carry on,' said the King. 'How's it going, sergeant?'

'No problems, Your Majesty. Had the engines running earlier. Sweet as a couple of nuts.' The King smiled. 'Just waiting upon Flight Lieutenant Fielden[1] Your Majesty,' the sergeant went on.

'Flight Lieutenant Fielden won't be coming, sergeant.'

'But –' The sergeant stopped short. He knew his place. But the look on his face showed his doubts. It was left to Churchill to express them. Turning his back on the sergeant, he said quietly, 'Surely you are not going to pilot her yourself, Sir? Not in these conditions?'

'Why not?' demanded the King. 'I'm a qualified pilot. And the fewer people who know what we are about, the better.'

'Yes, Sir, but –'

'Don't worry, Winnie,' the King interrupted him. 'I won't kill you.'

Outside the hangar the control tower was now silhouetted black against the greyness of approaching dawn.

The King climbed aboard the aeroplane and settled himself in the pilot's seat, running his eyes expertly over the compass, rev counter, airspeed indicator, altimeter and fuel gauge. He tried out the control column and rudder bar.

'We'll fly north-east after take-off,' he told Churchill, 'as though heading for Sandringham. Once we're out of sight of the control tower we'll turn south. I know the route to Le Bourget. I flew it the other way – Marseilles-Lyon-Le Bourget-Croydon – when I returned from Khartoum. When we touch down at Le Bourget I'll stay in the aeroplane while you get through to Fort Belvedere and see if there's any further news. Don't want someone recognising me and tipping off the newspapers, do we?'

The greyness of dawn strengthened into what was to pass, that December morning, for full daylight. The King pressed the self-starter and the twin 200-horse-power Gipsy engines came to life. He ran quickly through the customary checks, then signalled to the RAF men to remove the wheel chocks.

He taxied out of the hangar, glanced up at the wind stocking, and continued to taxi round until the Rapide pointed into the wind. He checked with the control tower that he was cleared for take-off. The Rapide surged forward, gathered speed and became airborne. From the windows of the tower the two controllers followed it with their eyes until the murk swallowed it up. 'Wonder what he's going to Sandringham for,' one of them pondered aloud.

'It was there he became King,' said the other. 'Perhaps he's going back there to abdicate.'

'He'll never abdicate,' replied his companion. 'Not him.'

The events of the next few days would prove him wrong. Indeed, the King, as he turned the Rapide south and headed for Le Bourget, had already made his decision. He knew now that there was no way he could marry Wallis and still remain on the throne. But he also felt, now more than ever, that he could not face the future without her. For love of her he was prepared to make any sacrifice.

Gauging distance flown from the Rapide's cruising speed of 132 mph, the King brought the aeroplane down below the cloud base once they were over the Channel. 'That looks like Le Touquet,' he said to Churchill as they flew over the French coast. Abbeville was next. 'Good,' said the King. 'All we have to do is follow the road and it will take us almost straight to Le Bourget.'

There was no problem about landing at Le Bourget. As arranged, the King remained hidden in the aeroplane while Churchill walked across to the airport buildings to put in a call to Fort Belvedere.

'No further news of Wallis, I'm afraid,' he reported on his return. 'But Monckton says that Baldwin has been trying to get in touch with you.'

'Bugger Baldwin,' the King retorted with feeling. He studied his map. 'No good making for Moulins. There's nowhere to land there, as far as I know. I think we'd better head for Lyon.'

At almost that very moment, as it happened, the Buick was running into the outskirts of Lyon, its occupants congratulating themselves that they had given their pursuers the slip. However, satisfaction was to be short-lived.

Alerted to the fact that their quarry had slipped away in the early hours of the morning, the newsmen snoozing in the hotel lobby at Blois had stampeded to the cars parked outside. Unlike the lone motor-cyclist, whose pursuit of the Buick had a more deadly purpose, most of them already knew that the Simpson party was making for Cannes. So they knew which road to follow and could take up the chase at a speed which was checked only by the atrocious weather conditions. They were helped too by the fact that the occupants of the Buick stopped at Moulins to order and eat breakfast.

The Duchess of Windsor's memoirs reveal that it was as they reached Lyon, some 360 kilometres further south, that the pursuing newspaper cars caught up with them again. She makes no mention of the fact that at the tail-end of the press cavalcade was a solitary motor-cycle.

If she did notice it, she had no reason to be concerned about it, of course. But those accompanying her had every reason for concern. Somehow they had to give it the slip. A fresh diversionary tactic was urgently necessary.

The opportunity came at Vienne, another 27 kilometres further on. The Buick came to a stop outside the world-famous Restaurant de la Pyramide, the newspaper cars screeching to a halt around it. Lord Brownlow and Wallis Simpson hurried inside. They sought out the proprietor and spoke with him, quickly, urgently. Pushing and jostling each other, reporters and photographers followed them in, just in time to see their quarry afforded the sanctuary of the proprietor's private rooms.

The Journal
(December 5)

I was becoming desperate. I still had no idea where Mrs S was heading, though I guessed it to be the French Riviera, Monte Carlo or somewhere similar, there to idle away her time until the crisis in England was resolved. Then she would either return to marry the King and be crowned as Queen Wallis or the King would abdicate and join her. Either course was unthinkable and would plunge the nation into chaos.

Only her death could prevent such a catastrophe. But time was fast running out. Any day, any hour even, could bring news of a decision which, whatever it was, would surely split the nation. I had to strike quickly.

The press having caught up with the Simpson party, the restaurant at Vienne was filled with noisy journalists busy ordering slap-up meals from waiters who looked surprised and bewildered at this sudden big influx of customers. There was no sign of Mrs S or Lord Brownlow. I spotted my new-found acquaintance from the Daily Record *and made my way to where he was sitting.*

'See you're still in disguise,' he quipped. 'You actually play golf?'

'Of course.'

'What handicap?'

'Two left hands,' I joked before asking, 'Where's la dame?'

He shrugged. 'Last I saw they were on their way upstairs. My guess is that they're gonna have a meal and a cat-nap. They had to be up around three to get the start they did. Must be about deadbeat by now. I know I am. Hungry too.' He clicked his fingers at a passing waiter. 'Ici, garçon.'

There was a sudden silence in the journalistic hubbub around me as Lord Brownlow entered accompanied by a man I had not seen before. From his dress and manner, the volatile gestures accompanying his words, he had to be French. Ears were pricked to hear what was being said. Not that there was much need for pricked ears. The gist of the conversation came over loud and clear. The Buick was low on petrol. The Frenchman was volunteering to show the chauffeur the way to the nearest garage. But there was something odd about the whole business, with everything being repeated two or even three times. Even my American friend seemed to think so. 'Another fine mess you've got me into, Stanley,' he quipped, sotto voce.

I knew what he meant. I had seen the American comedians, Laurel and Hardy, at the kinematograph theatre at Marble Arch. But I was also beginning to know the way Lord Brownlow's mind worked. This cross-talk act could be another of his tricks.

As he and the Frenchman walked out, still talking loudly about the Buick's lack of petrol, the hubbub resumed. 'Sit down and take the weight off your feet,' said the man from the Daily Record. *'Have something to eat. There's plenty of time. The lady's safe upstairs.'*

But if he and the others were satisfied that all was well in their journalistic world, I wasn't. 'Back in a minute,' I said and followed Lord Brownlow out.

I was in time to see him talking to the chauffeur. I could not hear what was said, but he was clearly giving instructions. The chauffeur and the Frenchman left the restaurant and headed towards where the Buick was parked.

I made a dash for the Norton. Wherever the Buick was going, I was fairly certain it was not simply to get petrol.[1] And I was determined to follow.

Then I stopped abruptly. There was someone standing beside my motor-bicycle, seemingly studying it. I could not see his face – he had his back to me – but his build was that of the bodyguard.

He turned – and so did I. Away from him. It worried me that he should be standing so close to the Norton as though suspicious of it. If he was suspicious, he might challenge me if I went near it. Even if I didn't, he might spot my black leather outfit at any moment and guess I was its owner.

There was a car parked where I was standing. I tried the door. It was unlocked. I opened it, reached inside to lay the golf-bag on the rear seat and climbed behind the steering-wheel out of his view.

Ahead of me, the Buick was moving off. And now I had no way of following. Then I saw that the car in which I had taken refuge still had its ignition key in place.

I turned the key and pressed the self-starter. The engine declined to fire. The car was French, a Citroen, small and inconspicuous, left-hand drive, its controls unfamiliar to me, but the two levers mounted on the steering-wheel presumably controlled the ignition and mixture. I adjusted them slightly and tried again. This time the engine came to life. I engaged the gear lever, took off the hand-brake and pulled away in pursuit of the Buick.

I was just in time to see it turn left. Then the engine of my borrowed car decided to stall on me. By the time I had it going again and turned the corner there was no sign of the Buick. I spent the next few minutes driving up and down a succession of cobbled side-streets in the hope of spotting it, but without success.

I found myself at the town centre. Convinced that the Buick had not gone simply in search of petrol, I stopped and studied the direction signs. Ever since Dieppe, though there had been diversions along the way, the Buick had been heading steadily south. So of the five roads which met at Vienne, the odds were that they would take the N7 to Valence and Avignon. And that was the road I took.

It was still sleeting, but less heavily. I located the control for the windscreen wiper and got it going. The inside of the screen was misting up. I wiped a clear patch with my hand and rolled down the window a few inches. I looked at the fuel gauge. Plenty of petrol. I didn't know whether I was ahead or behind the Buick or even for certain that I was on the right road. I pushed the accelerator pedal almost to the floorboards and drove flat out.

I caught up with the Buick at a crossroads about twenty-five kilometres south of Vienne, where a minor road crosses the main N7. Caught up? I was nearly in collision with it. Due to the bad visibility I didn't see it until I was almost upon it and I certainly didn't expect it to be emerging from a side road on my right. It had presumably taken the secondary road which runs parallel with the N7. It had its side lights on and it was these which alerted me. Instinctively I braked. The Citroen skidded on the sleet-slippery surface of the road. I turned into the skid, shot across the road, missed the bonnet of the Buick by a hair's-breadth and regained my correct side of the road in the nick of time to avoid being ploughed under by a lorry coming the other way. Recovering my composure, I looked in the driving-mirror and saw the lights of the Buick following me along the N7.

Quite suddenly I realised that I had been going the wrong way about things. I had waited upon opportunity and opportunity had not served me well. It was time to create my own opportunity. The lights of the Buick vanished into the murk behind me as I again pushed the accelerator to the floorboards. There were less than two hours of uncertain daylight left in which to put my new plan into operation.

Another thirty kilometres brought me to Valence. Mrs S might stop there for the night, but I doubted it. Unless I missed my guess, she was heading for somewhere on the Riviera. So I drove on towards Avignon.

I found what I was looking for just south of Montelimar, a stretch of road running straight and true through an area of unhedged, almost treeless heathland. I brought the car to a halt, reached behind me for the Mannlicher, inserted a clip of ammunition, got out of the car and ran across to the other side of the road. I climbed the heathland until I had a clear view of the direction from which I had come. I took a trial sighting and waited for the Buick to catch up with me.

My plan was simple. I would take out one of the tyres. Those inside would hardly hear the shot above the sound of the engine. Even if they did, they would put it down to a puncture. The Buick would be forced to stop for a wheel change. With any luck, Mrs S would get out to stretch her legs. And that would be the last thing she did in this world.

It was still sleeting, chilling my hands and face, running in rivulets down my leathers. The light, such as it was, was fading further. I realised that I had given no thought to making a getaway after the deed was done. Indeed, the question of a getaway no longer seemed so important. The important thing was to save the King from the consequences of his folly, whatever the *price I had to pay. Still, better not to pay it if possible. A quick dash to the stolen car while the other occupants of the Buick were still confused by what had happened and I could get away scot-free. If one of them tried to tackle me, too bad for him. I didn't want to kill anyone other than Mrs S, but I would if I had to.*

Bone-weary as I was, my concentration had waivered momentarily. The noise of an engine jerked me back to immediate reality. But it was only another lorry, northbound. My whole being felt frozen. I gripped the Mannlicher with my knees while I rubbed my hands together to restore circulation. Where the devil was the Buick? If Mrs S was much longer, if the cold really ate into me, I wouldn't like to guarantee my marksmanship. It was like being in Scotland, I thought, waiting to draw a bead on a twelve-pointer.

Another engine, a car this time and going in the right direction. But not the Buick. A nip of cognac. that was what I needed. I fumbled for the flask, put it to my lips and took a quick sip.

Another car went past; and another. Then silence again except for the patter of sleet on my leathers. Wet beaded the barrel of the rifle. Then another car came into view quite suddenly from the right direction, emerging from the murk with its outline hazed and indefinite. I screwed up my eyes in an attempt to bring it more sharply into focus.

It was the Buick.

I cuddled the stock of the Mannlicher more tightly into my shoulder, sighted on the front offside wheel, moving the rifle to keep pace with the Buick as it came towards me. I had picked my spot well so that it needed only a minimum of movement on my part to hold my aim as the Buick came on. Aiming fractionally ahead to compensate for its speed, I squeezed the trigger.

The Buick slewed sideways as the bullet found its mark and the offside front tyre collapsed.

In the Nick of Time
(December 5)

At Lyon the King again remained out of sight in the Rapide while Churchill went into the airport buildings to put another call through to Fort Belvedere. He was gone a long time, so long that the King became increasingly worried and impatient. He could hardly restrain himself when Churchill finally returned bearing a steaming mug in either hand.

'Thought we could do with some hot coffee,' he said, passing the mugs up to the King before climbing aboard.

'Hang the coffee,' snapped the King. 'What news?'

Churchill settled himself in his seat and took one of the mugs from the King. 'Sorry to have been so long,' he apologised, 'but I had a devil of a job getting through. Anyhow, there's been another call from Mrs Harris. They're at a place called Vienne. She was calling from a restaurant there – the Pyramid something or other.'

The King set his coffee mug aside and reached for the map. 'Vienne? Ah, here it is. Due south of here. About twenty-five to thirty kilometres. If we get a car, we might catch them before they leave again.' He started to get out of his seat.

'I'm afraid not, Sir,' Churchill said. 'I telephoned the restaurant and they've already left.' He chuckled. 'Had a job winkling it out of them. Seemed to think I was some sort of newspaper johnny. Took a few minutes to convince them I wasn't.'

'How long ago did they leave?' the King asked.

'I gathered they had only just left, Sir.'

'Say half an hour. The N7 is a good road.' He traced it on the map with his finger. 'They'll be well on their way to Valence by now. Then about another 140-150 kilometres to Avignon. Flying, we'll overtake them long before that. Unfortunately, I don't know anywhere to land at Avignon. Have to go on to Marseilles. I know there's an airfield there. Landed there on my way back from Khartoum.'

'Is that on their route?' Churchill queried.

'No,' the King said, 'but we'll be well ahead of them by then. If we can get a car at Marseilles we can cut back to Aix-en-Provence and link up with them there.' He put the map away.

'Don't forget your coffee, Sir,' Churchill reminded him.

The King took a quick sip. 'Too hot,' he said. 'Waste of time.' He passed the mug over to Churchill. 'Get rid of that for me, Winnie. Time we were airborne.'

He pressed the self-starter and the twin engines of the Rapide roared into life. He re-fastened his flying helmet and gestured to Churchill to do the same. Then he taxied round into the wind and within seconds they were airborne again, banking round to continue south. There was a low cloud base. The King flew through it and above it until they were clear of the airfield, then descended below it.

'A trifle low, aren't we, Sir?' Churchill inquired, apprehensively.

'Have to follow the road,' the King replied. 'Don't worry, Winnie. I've often flown as low as this.'

'Watch out for church steeples,' Churchill cautioned.

Ten minutes at the Rapide's cruising speed of 132 mph brought them to a small town. 'That should be Vienne,' the King said. 'Check the map, will you?'

Churchill did so. 'I'd say you're right, Sir.'

'Keep an eye on the road, will you? Say if you spot anything that looks like them. They're in a Buick.'

Churchill nodded.

They continued to fly south, following the N7, flying so low at times that on one occasion Churchill could even see the horrified look on the face of a bicyclist as he glimpsed the Rapide zooming towards him through the sleet. They overtook several vehicles as they flew, but not the Buick. When there was still no sight of it another fifteen or twenty minutes later the King muttered, 'Where the devil are they? We should have spotted them by now.'

Another huddle of rooftops loomed up ahead. 'Where's that?' the King asked.

Churchill studied the map. 'Seems to be a place called Tain l'Heritage.' Within minutes they were over a small cathedral town. 'Valence, I think,' said Churchill.

They continued to fly low, the King following the road and Churchill tracing their route on the map. 'Monte-limar,' he announced shortly.

Hardly had Montelimar been left behind than he spoke again. 'There, Sir – isn't that a Buick?'

'Looks very like one,' said the King.

Even as he spoke the car slewed suddenly across the road.

'Something's wrong,' said the King.

They watched as the car slowed, pulled back to its correct side of the road and coasted to a standstill.

'Looks as though they've had a puncture,' said Churchill. Almost at once he spoke again on a note of urgency. 'What's that?'

'What? Where?' the King demanded.

But by this time they had overflown the Buick. Churchill twisted in his seat, looking down and back. That sense of danger which had served him so well in younger days, in South Africa and elsewhere, was suddenly with him again. 'Turn round,' he said urgently.

'I can't just turn the damned thing round,' the King retorted, banking even as he spoke. 'For heaven's sake, what is it, Winnie?'

'Someone with a gun.'

'A gun? Where?'

'Back there,' said Churchill as the Rapide completed its turn. 'Near the Buick. Can't see him now.'

By now the Buick had disgorged its occupants. Instinctively they ducked as the Rapide roared low

overhead. The King put the aeroplane into another tight
turn. The wind-blown sleet cleared momentarily to give
him and Churchill a clear view of the scene below.

The King said, 'That's Wallis –'

'Over there, Sir,' Churchill cut in on him. 'Look.'

Jerking his head round, the King saw the solitary figure
on the far side of the road, gun to shoulder. 'He's shooting
at them. Why don't they stay in the car, the fools.' He
pushed the control column forwards and sideways.
Desperately low already, the Rapide dived lower still,
banking, its under-carriage only feet above the Buick as it
roared across the N7. The figure on the heath looked up,
startled, and for a split second the King had a fleeting
glimpse of a white face in a shiny surround of black
leather.

In the nick of time, as the Rapide hurtled towards it so
low that its under-carriage threatened decapitation, the
figure threw itself to the ground. The King hauled
desperately on the control column as it seemed that the
Rapide itself must crash. Its landing wheels were actually
brushing the undergrowth before the aeroplane responded, its nose coming up into a steep climb.

Churchill was obliged to hang on to his seat with both
hands as the King banked almost on one wingtip to roar
back towards where the figure in black was now running
down the slope of the heath and along the road. As the
Rapide levelled out, he grabbed the King's arm and
pointed. 'He's making for that other car.'

Below them, those with the Buick had not yet noticed
the fleeing figure. All eyes were focused on the aeroplane
again flashing towards them.

'Get down,' shouted Lord Brownlow.

Even as he said it, he bundled Wallis Simpson to the
ground in the shadow of the Buick, shielding her with his
own body as the Rapide roared back across the N7 and
vanished, climbing, into the murk. It was only as he
helped her to her feet again that he and those with him
spotted the running figure. He called out.

The running figure stopped, turned, and now for the
first time they saw the rifle. Even as Brownlow pushed

Wallis Simpson back into the Buick, a shot rang out. The bullet flew high and wide. Then the figure was on the move again, racing towards a car parked some two hundred yards ahead of the Buick. Before any of those in the party could react, the running figure had reached the car, scrambled in and the car was pulling away.

Wallis Simpson, her face deathly pale, started to say something, but her words were lost in the roar of aeroplane engines as the Rapide came into view again, higher this time. They watched as it banked and flew away to the south. 'Let's get this wheel changed,' ordered Lord Brownlow as it disappeared from view.

While the men in the party worked to get the Buick roadworthy again, the Rapide continued to fly south, again coming down low to follow the route of the N7.

'I thought for a moment back there that we were going to crash,' Churchill ventured to say.

The King gave a wintry smile. 'So did I, Winnie. So did I.'

'If I may say so, Sir, you're still rather low.'

'Got to be in this light if I'm to follow the road. I want to catch that damned car.'

Puzzled, Churchill said, 'But they're behind us, Sir.'

'Not the Buick, Winnie – that other one. Ah, there it is now.'

Churchill looked down and saw the speeding car. 'Are you sure it's the same one, Sir?'

'Pretty sure. Check the map, will you, and tell me what place comes next.'

Churchill did as he was bid. 'Somewhere called Orange, Sir.' He pronounced it in the English fashion.

By now the aeroplane was ahead of the car, leaving it further and further behind. In seconds it was lost to view.

'Any side roads where he might turn off?' the King asked.

Churchill consulted the map. 'None that I can see.'

Good,' said the King, grimly.

The port wing of the aeroplane dropped as he banked. The turn completed, they were flying back the way they had come. Lower and lower they flew until the under-carriage was barely ten feet above the surface of the road.

'May I ask, Sir, what you intend to do?' Churchill inquired.

'I'm going to land in front of the bloody thing, that's what,' retorted the King.

The Journal
December 5–6)

Under my breath I damned the aeroplane as I fled the scene of my intended kill. But for its sudden and unexpected appearance I would have had Mrs S stone cold. Where had it come from? What in the world was it doing there? There had been no sign of it previously. Yet suddenly there it was, flashing across the road, heading straight for me. If I had not thrown myself flat it would have taken my head off. I had expected it to crash behind me, but it hadn't. Instead, it had zoomed up, then come back for another try.

I am sorry to confess that at the moment my sang-froid deserted me. Not to mince words, I panicked. If I had stayed cool I might still have picked off Mrs S. Instead of which, I had fled for the car, discharging a second shot, wild and useless, to prevent pursuit. Despite all my earlier resolution, my own life, at that moment, had seemed more important than Mrs Simpson's death. I was not the potential martyr I had thought myself to be.

I was still panic-stricken as I drove off, grating through the gears, pushing the accelerator to the floorboards until the speedometer flickered between 90 and 100 kilometres an hour. An oncoming car rushed towards me out of the murk, its horn blaring as it swerved wildly across the road and flashed past. I had forgotten I was in France. I should be driving on the right. I swung across the road and switched on the headlamps. Sleet glittered in the glare of yellow light. In the nick of time I spotted the rear lights of a lorry ahead of me. I pulled out to overtake, almost into the path of an oncoming car. We passed each other with no more than the thickness of a cigarette paper to spare.

Crossroads loomed up. I flashed across them. I knew I was driving much too fast, in that light, in those weather conditions, but my only thought was to get as far away as quickly as possible.

Ahead of me, out of the darkening murk, a monstrous object suddenly appeared. It seemed to take up the whole road. At first I thought it was some sort of giant agricultural vehicle.

It wasn't.

It was an aeroplane.

Actually on the road, its wings spanning almost the whole width of the road.

I jammed hard on the brake. I don't know whether the aeroplane was moving or stationary. The Citroen continued to slide towards it. I was going to hit it. I spun the steering-wheel, hoping to swerve round it. The tip of its lower wing continued to rush towards me. Instinctively I ducked. The Citroen hit the verge, careered across it, dropped, turned over. My body jerked forward and my head cracked against the steering-wheel.

I don't think I could have been out for more than a few minutes. But I continued to lie there on my side, dazed, with neither the strength nor the inclination to move. As from a great way off I heard a man's voice say, 'Watch out for his gun.'

Another voice said, 'I don't think he's in any condition to use a gun.'

There was the sound of grating metal as the offside door of the car was forced open. The beam of a flashlamp shone down on me.

I felt myself being pulled and lifted.

'Think you can stand up?' a voice asked.

With help, I struggled to my feet. 'Try to walk,' someone said.

I realised then that there were two of them. They stood either side of me, each grasping an arm, steadying me as I took a few uncertain steps.

'Up you go.' One pulling, the other pushing, they helped me into the aeroplane. The cabin lights were dim. They lowered me into a seat. 'Wiggle your fingers,' a voice said. 'Good. Now the other hand. Try lifting your leg. Now the other. Don't think you've broken anything.'

'That's a nasty cut on the face,' a second voice said.

'I'll get the first-aid kit. Be taking that helmet off.'

Fingers fumbled with the strap beneath my chin and the helmet came off. I heard someone say 'Good Lord' and a face came into focus for the first time. It was a face I had seen before, once or twice in the flesh, many times in the newspapers.

'Mr Churchill,' I exclaimed.

The other man returned with the first-aid kit and I recognised him too. I struggled to get out of my seat, but was still too shaken to succeed. 'Sit still,' he said.

'I'm sorry to cause you all this trouble, Your Majesty,' I apologised.

He stood looking down at me, his eyes screwed up in an effort of concentration. His face wore a curious expression as though he was searching his memory for something that eluded him.

'Don't I know you?' he said.

In a sense, he did. He had once spent a weekend as my parents' house guest. But that was years ago. I had been – how old? – thirteen – fourteen. I had grown up since then; changed a lot. He couldn't possibly remember.

'You know my parents, Your Majesty.'

He shook his head, puzzled. 'No, it isn't that.'

Mr Churchill said, 'We can't stay here, Sir. In the dark something could crash into us at any moment.'

'Yes, I know.' The King spoke as though his mind was still on something else. 'See to that cut,' he said.

He went forward to the controls, leaving Mr Churchill to clean my cut with a piece of lint and dab it with iodine. The iodine stung like the devil. The noise of the engines rose to a climax and the aeroplane surged forward. Mr Churchill pressed a pad of lint on the cut and taped it in place with some sticky plaster. I felt us become airborne.

For a private aeroplane, if that's what it was, the cabin was pretty spacious. It was a type I had flown in before. One of the civil airlines used it – or something like it – for flights between London and Paris. It had seats for six. Mr Churchill sat down, his body angled towards me.

'You've got a lot of explaining to do.'

'I know,' I said.

'We've got the gun. Precisely what game were you after?'

I didn't answer.

He put the question more directly. 'What did you hope to achieve by shooting Mrs Simpson?'

I still felt lightheaded. 'God save the King,' I said.

'From Mrs Simpson?' he asked.

'From abdicating,' I said. 'What will happen to me?' I asked.

'That depends upon His Majesty.' He stood up and moved away to join the King at the controls.

I think I was still in shock following the accident. Certainly my mind and body were alike exhausted. I don't know whether I slept or fainted. Either way, the aeroplane was at rest, its engines silent, when I next opened my eyes. The King was shaking me by the shoulder and saying, 'Wake up.'

'Are we in England?' I asked.

'No,' he said. 'Marseilles.' He turned to Mr Churchill. 'See if you can hire a car, Winnie. I don't want to be spotted if it can possibly be helped. And see if you can get through to the Fort again; find out if they've heard anything more from Lord Brownlow.'

Churchill said, 'Sir, is it wise –' He stopped abruptly, then said, 'As you wish, Sir,' and clambered awkwardly out of the aeroplane.

The King sat down opposite, staring at me in silence for a moment, a frown creasing his forehead. Then he shook his head as though something still eluded him. Finally he said, 'Did you really intend to kill Mrs Simpson?'

I could hardly deny it, so I said nothing.

'But why?' he asked.

'I wanted you to remain on the throne, Sir.'

'And you thought that with Mrs Simpson dead ...' His voice trailed away.

I could restrain myself no longer. Words spurted from me as steam does from a boiling kettle. 'Sir, you must not abdicate. You are the King. It is your duty to remain on the throne.'

'Duty?' He gave an odd little smile. 'I seem to have heard that before.' He shook his head. 'I don't think I'm the stuff of which kings are made. My heart isn't in it.'

'You're wrong, Sir. Terribly, terribly wrong. Sir, I urge you – beg you – please, please, give up Mrs Simpson.'

'That I could never do. Does no one understand – I love her?'

'Then go on loving her. Let her be your mistress. No one will mind that.'

'That would be hypocrisy,' said the King, 'and so grossly unfair to her. If I did that, I would be a king without honour.'

'You must not abdicate, Sir,' I insisted.

'I fear it is too late to do anything else.'

Silence fell between us. Presently the King said, 'I know your father. A fine man. It would be a sad thing if one of my last actions as King was to shame him. The difficulty is the police –'

'The police!' I repeated, interrupting him. 'But they don't know anything about me.'

'I think you will find that they do. More than they have told me, I imagine.'

'Does that mean I'll go to prison?'

He pursed his lips. 'We'll see.'

I didn't want to go to prison. Not so much for myself, but for the shame, as the King had said, that it would bring on my father and my family. But I had too much pride to beg even on that account.

The King said, 'There may be –' He broke off as Mr Churchill climbed back into the aeroplane. 'Well?' he asked him.

'I managed to get a car, Sir.'

'Did you get through to the Fort?'

'I did, Sir. No further word from Lord Brownlow, I'm afraid. But there's been a call from the Duke of York. He needs to see you urgently, he said.'

'Hang – I clean forgot,' the King said. 'I promised to see him, then had to put him off. They didn't tell him anything about this, did they?'

Churchill shook his head. 'Simply that you would contact him tomorrow.'

'What must he think of me? I seem to be letting him down rather badly. I must see him as soon as we get back and try to get everything straightened out.' He made an effort at smiling. 'Wonder how he'll take to the idea of being King. He won't like it, but he'll do it. And make a good job of it – him and that sweet little wife of his.'

'Then you've made up your mind, Sir?' Mr Churchill asked.

'You might say that I've had it made up for me.' There was a touch of bitterness to his voice. He stood up. 'Time we were off.'

'You're sure it's wise to go to Cannes, Sir?' Mr Churchill asked.

'It's not a question of being wise,' the King said. 'I have to –' He stopped, then said, 'Don't worry so, Winnie. We'll be there by midnight. Back here by dawn. Back at the Fort by lunch time *or shortly after and no one any the wiser.'* He went through to the cockpit and returned with a map. *'Best plan is to head for Aix-en-Provence and then follow the N7. It's a longer route, but a better road. We must arrange for the plane to be serviced and refuelled while we are gone.'*

'What about –' Mr Churchill nodded in my direction.

'Ah, yes,' the King said. He turned back to where I was still sitting. *'I think you should come with us.'*

The car Mr Churchill had managed to hire was a Delage. The King sat in it with me, keeping out of sight, familiarising himself with the controls, while Mr Churchill went off to arrange about the aeroplane. As the minutes ticked away he became increasingly restless, impatient to be gone.

'Sorry for the delay, Sir,' Mr Churchill apologised on his return. *'Had something of a job convincing them that they'd get their money in the fullness of time.'*

'So long as you didn't mention me,' the King said.

'Of course not, Sir.'

'Don't want this getting into the newspapers,' the King muttered as Mr Churchill climbed in beside him.

I was sitting in the back. The King proved himself an excellent driver and, despite the dark and the bad weather, we reached Aix-en-Provence in well under the hour. We turned on to the main road which led to Fréjus and through Fréjus to Cannes. Mr Churchill had a map on his lap and followed the route with the aid of a small flashlamp. *'St Maximin,'* he announced as we flashed through. *'Brignoles coming up. That's about halfway.'*

This was a part of France I knew well from holidays spent on the Riviera. I remember stopping at Brignoles for a meal one year. It had been a day of bright sunshine with the men in blazers or alpaca jackets and the women in light summer frocks. Now it was a winter's night, an hour short of midnight, damp and cold, the streets deserted.

No, not quite deserted, it seemed. Not far from the town centre we came upon a stationary car, its headlamps full on so as to illuminate a public telephone fixed to a wall and a man who stood there pounding the telephone box with his fist in seeming frustration. As we drew level the King braked unexpectedly. *'I'm sure that's Perry,'* he exclaimed.

He backed up, pulled in behind the parked car and jumped out, *leaving the door of the Delage open. The angry shouting of the man at the telephone could be heard clearly in the otherwise silent street. The King walked over to him and tapped him on the shoulder.*

'Can I be of assistance?' I heard him say.[1]

'Blasted Froggies have no idea how to run a decent telephone system,' the man snapped. He turned – and his jaw sagged noticeably. 'Your Majesty,' he exclaimed. 'How in the world –'

The rest of what he said was lost in the click-clack of heels as Wallis Simpson jumped out of the other car and ran towards the King.

'David,' I heard her exclaim. 'Is it really you?'

They embraced. Lord Brownlow – for that's who it was – replaced the telephone and moved discreetly away. The King and Wallis Simpson stayed there in the glare of the headlamps, their hands joined, their heads close.

Lord Brownlow walked back to the Delage and Mr Churchill wound down the window on his side. The two of them exchanged a few words.

The King returned to the open door on the driver's side, leaned over and crooked a finger at me. 'Come with me,' he said.

I couldn't imagine what he wanted. Lord Brownlow made as though to accompany us.

'Not you, Perry,' the King said. 'This won't take a minute and then you can be on your way again.'

I followed him to the Buick.

'I think you know Mrs Simpson,' he said. He gave that quizzical little smile of his. 'At least by sight.' He turned towards her. 'This is the person I've been telling you about, Wallis.'

She studied me closely, coolly. 'I must say you don't look the type,' she said.

I didn't know what to say. I gave an embarrassed shake of the head and lowered my eyes.

'Do you think me so very wicked?' she asked.

Wicked? Hardly. A lot of other things perhaps, but not that.

'I wanted the King to stay King,' I said.

'I don't suppose you will believe me,' she said, 'but so do I.' I raised my head and looked at her again. I had to say it.

'With you as Queen.'

'I had –' She stopped, shaking her head. 'No,' she said. 'I know

now that that is not possible.' She looked at the King. 'Without me.'

He made a grimace, half smile, half bitterness. 'Without you, I could never be King, Wallis. No,' he went on, raising a hand to check her as she was about to say something more. 'My mind is made up.'

It was difficult to be sure in the light of the Buick's headlamps, but I thought her eyes brimmed with tears. Until then, she had been only a target to be brought down. I had felt nothing for her, not even contempt. But now, seeing her close up, talking to her, I felt only immense pity for her and for the King. Two people in love, trapped by the intensity of their own emotions.

'I'm sorry for what I tried to do,' I said.

'Wait in the car, will you?' the King said to me. 'And ask Lord Brownlow to join us.'

I did as he said. Lord Brownlow rejoined them and the three of them stood talking for a few minutes. Then Lord Brownlow climbed back into the Buick. Its headlamps died. A minute later, perhaps two, I heard a car door slam. The Buick's engines started up, the headlamps came on again and it pulled away. The King stood looking after it until long after it was out of sight. Then he returned to the Delage.

It must have been around two o'clock in the morning when we arrived back at Marseilles. We catnapped in the car until first light. Then, with the King's aeroplane serviced and refuelled, we took off for London. It was just under five hours later, around lunch time, when we touched down at the Aerodrome, Croydon. The roar of the aeroplane's engines died away and a minute or two later the King came through to the passenger compartment where I was sitting.

'Now what are we going to do about you?' he said, musingly.

Memory of Things Past
(December 6–7)

All that Sunday the Duke of York remained within earshot of the telephone, awaiting the expected call from his elder brother. Even at this late hour, if they met and talked, he hoped he might prevail upon him to renounce Mrs Simpson. But the morning passed and afternoon became evening with still no word from the King.

Finally, he could stand the waiting no longer. He picked up the telephone and himself called the King. To his amazement and dismay he was told, 'The King is in conference and will speak to you later.'

The 'conference', if such it could be called, was in the library at Fort Belvedere. Initially, there were only three people present in addition to the King. Later they would be joined by a fourth.

With no knowledge of what had been going on in France, Chief Superintendent Sinclair had been personally supervising the hunt in the Windsor area when he received word that he should contact Fort Belvedere immediately. He did so and found himself connected with the King.

'How goes it with your inquiries, Chief Superintendent?' The crisis over, his mind at ease, his decision made concerning that other crisis still to be resolved, the King could not resist a small joke.

'We have not yet arrested the suspect, but we know who it is. Every available man is on the look-out. It can be only a matter of time, Sir.'

'You can call your men off and send them home. The suspect is in custody.'

'But where? How? Why wasn't I informed?' Puzzled, flummoxed for once in his life, Sinclair realised too late that he had omitted the obligatory 'Sir'.

'I am informing you now, Chief Superintendent,' the King continued to joke.

'I don't understand, Sir.'

'Be at the Fort at seven o'clock and I'll explain everything.'

At Keston Castle the 12th Duke had been even more surprised to receive a telephone call requiring both him and the Duchess to wait upon the King at seven o'clock that evening. 'What the deuce can he want of us?' he demanded of his wife.

'I can't possibly imagine.'

The Duchess kept her voice level though her thoughts were racing. She could think of one possibility. So distressing was the possibility that what the King actually had to say, a shock though as it was, came as something of a relief.

He saw the Duke and Duchess first, then Chief Superintendent Sinclair, separately. Now the four of them were together in the library. The King crossed to the far door and opened it.

'You can come in now, Lady Davina.'

She looked tired and dejected, her oval face very pale in contrast to the black leather of her motor-cycle outfit, a length of plaster covering the cut sustained when the Citroen overturned. Her mouth quivered as she fled across the room and threw herself into the arms of the Duchess.

'Oh, Mummy, Mummy, I don't know what came over me.'

'I should think not,' rumbled the Duke. 'Silly little –' He stopped in time to avoid saying a word not to be used in front of the King. 'Your Majesty,' he said. 'On behalf of my daughter, on behalf of the family, I tender you –'

'Enough,' said the King. 'It's over; done with. Lady Davina –'

Still clutching her mother, the daughter turned a tear-stained face towards him.

The King gestured towards Sinclair. 'This is Chief Superintendent Sinclair of Scotland Yard. He wants to arrest you.'

The Duchess brought her hand to her mouth. 'Oh no.' She began to weep.

Her daughter said, 'Please don't, Mummy.' She detached herself from her mother's embrace, her tear-stained face slightly defiant. 'I haven't actually killed anyone,' she said. 'So you won't hang me. But I suppose I'll have to go to prison.'

'No,' exclaimed the Duchess. 'David, you can't.'

The use of the King's name caused her husband to look at her aghast. But he said nothing. Regaining her composure, the Duchess said, 'Sir, you promised –'

'I know,' the King interrupted her. He looked from her to her daughter. 'Sending you to prison would be unfair on your family. It would tarnish their good name. As King, I cannot interfere with the course of justice –' Outside the King's range of vision, Chief Superintendent Sinclair's face wore a slightly cynical expression. Then it became expressionless as the King continued ' – but having discussed the matter with the Chief Superintendent, he agrees that no useful purpose would be served by bringing charges against you. Indeed, it would possibly involve calling the King as a witness and that would hardly be proper. Isn't that so, Chief Superintendent?'

'As you say, Your Majesty.' Sinclair's voice was flat and non-committal.

'Then I think that's all, Chief Superintendent,' the King said. 'You have my permission to withdraw.'

Sinclair bowed as he withdrew, collected his coat, gloves and bowler hat from an ante-room and went out to where Sergeant Thompson was waiting for him in the car.

'Do we know where she is, sir?' Thompson asked. 'Are we going to arrest her?'

'She's back in there, sergeant, and no, we're not,' Sinclair snapped.

'I don't understand, sir. What's she doing in there? Why

aren't we going to arrest her? She's not going to be allowed to get away with it?'

'Yes, sergeant,' Sinclair retorted, 'she's going to get away with it. And if you don't think she should, perhaps you'd like to go back in there and try telling the King.'

'No, sir. Of course not,' Thompson mumbled as they drove off.

A few minutes later the Duke and Duchess left also, the daughter with them. Alone again, the King crossed to the telephone and asked to be put through to Cannes. He had already spoken with Wallis earlier in the day, assuring himself that she had reached the Villa Lou Viei safely, but he felt the need to hear her voice again. Besides, having reached his decision, he wanted the woman he loved to be the first to know. But when her voice came over the telephone, urging him to fight to stay on the throne, her spirit proved too strong for him and he kept his decision to himself. And still he did not telephone his brother.

The Duke of York had originally planned to return to London on the Monday. Instead, cancelling his appointments, he stayed on at Royal Lodge, every moment awaiting the long-expected call from the King. It came – finally – at ten minutes to seven.

'You'd better come and see me after dinner, Bertie,' the King said.

'B-blow dinner, David.' Pent-up emotion brought on the younger brother's stammer. 'I'll come at once.'

It took him only a few minutes to drive from Royal Lodge to Fort Belvedere. Finally face to face with his brother, he tried to reason with him, pleading with him to renounce Mrs Simpson and remain on the throne.

'It's no good, Bertie,' said the King. 'My mind is made up. I will never renounce Wallis.' The die cast, the King's mood lightened and his mouth twisted into the familiar quizzical smile. 'Don't look so downhearted, Bertie. You're going to be King in my place.'

'I – I don't want to be King, David.'

'No one wants to be King,' his brother joked. Then, more seriously, he went on, 'But some are cut out to make a better job of it than others. And you'll make a damned good job of it, Bertie – you'll see.'

Moved by the emotion of the moment, the two brothers, the one who would soon be King no more and the other who would reign in his stead, embraced each other.

The Duke of York said as they walked to his car, 'This means that one day Lilibet[1] will be Queen. I know one thing – I'll take good care she doesn't come to the throne as unprepared as I am.'

His brother had gone, dinner was over and the King was alone with his thoughts when an unexpected visitor was announced.

'I had to come and thank you, David,' said the Duchess, her gloved hand resting lightly on the King's arm. 'It was most generous of you.'

'I could hardly let the daughter of an old and dear friend go to prison. How old is she?'

'Nineteen.'

'Little more than a child.'

'You didn't think me a child at that age.'

'No.' The King smiled. 'But she isn't like you, is she?'

'Not really.'

The King wanted the conversation to end, but did not wish to seem rude. This was no time for a memory of things past. 'Takes more after her father, I imagine,' he said.

'Exactly like her father,' the Duchess replied. 'Self-willed, wants things her own way, inclined to rush ahead without counting the cost.'

'She doesn't take after him in looks.'

'You think not?' She didn't wait for him to reply, but went on, 'But I mustn't detain you, David. I'm sure you have more important things to attend to. I just wanted to thank you – and say goodbye. We probably won't ever see each other again. You're going to abdicate, aren't you?'

The King nodded. 'There's nothing else I can do. Come, I'll see you to your car.'

He walked outside with her and handed her into the car. The Duchess lowered the window, but neither spoke for fear that her chauffeur might overhear. Then, as the car was pulling away, the King called out, 'Nineteen did you say?'

She did not reply. Or if she did, the King failed to hear it above the noise of the engine and the crunch of wheels on gravel.

The Duchess, as she was driven away, retreated into a corner of the rear compartment so that the chauffeur should not see her reflection in his mirror. Tears trickled down her cheeks. But it seemed that her mouth smiled.

The Letter

Four days later, on December 10, 1936 – the King signed the Instrument of Abdication in the presence of his three brothers, the Dukes of York, Gloucester and Kent. Parliament ratified it the following day and the Duke of York was proclaimed as the new King George VI. That evening, after dark, the ex-King, now Duke of Windsor, drove to Portsmouth where the destroyer *Fury* waited to carry him out of the country. The following year, on June 3, he married Wallis Simpson, or Wallis Warfield as she preferred to be known on her wedding day. And that would have been the end of this book but for a letter penned half a century later by a woman dying from cancer.

The letter, which reached me along with the typescript copy of the book which I had left with her, was in handwriting so shaky that in parts it was almost illegible; quite unlike the neat tight penmanship of the Journal she had written all those years before.

I am arranging for this letter to be sent to you only when I am dead (she wrote), and death is now only a few days away. My parents also being dead, I cannot see that any harm can come from publishing what you are pleased to call my 'Journal'. As a book it may well make a great deal of money and, as you will see from the amended agreement, I would like my share to go to the hospice. The staff here have done so much to ease the last few months of my time on earth.

I wrote the Journal following my return from France. I had no thought that it would ever be published, of course. I simply wanted to clear my mind – perhaps rid myself of a sense of guilt – by setting things down on paper. Then something happened which caused me to leave the Journal unfinished.

It was the night of the King's broadcast. Only now he was the ex-King, of course. I listened to him on the wireless with mixed emotions. I felt sorry for him, embarrassed for him and angry with him.

The King – somehow I still thought of him as King – had just reached that bit about not having the matchless blessing of a wife and children when Mummy hurried from the room. That surprised me and as soon as the broadcast was over I went upstairs to see her. She was sitting at her dressing-table, her head in her hands, sobbing. I asked her what was wrong. She raised her face. She looked desperately unhappy. 'Is it the King?' I asked.

She nodded and, without speaking, unlocked her jewel box, opened one of the drawers and brought out an old sepia photograph of a young man in officer's uniform. I turned it over. On the back was written *All my love – David – 1916*. Then she told me how they had met during the Great War and become lovers.

'But you were married,' I accused her.

'I was very young,' she said, 'as you are now. And foolish – as you have been – but in different fashion. We were living in London and because of the war your – the Duke was away a great deal.' There was something odd in the way she said it. I could see her face reflected in the dressing-table mirror and, above and behind it, my own. All at once I knew what it was that had so puzzled the King when he bathed my cut on the aeroplane.

'Nineteen-sixteen,' I said. 'The year before I was born.'

'Yes,' she said so softly that it almost wasn't a word at all.

'Is that why you called me Davina?'

She nodded.

'Does Papa know?'

'Of course not,' she said. 'He thinks –' She didn't finish the sentence.

'Does the King?' I asked.

'He didn't,' she said, 'but I think he does now.'

There was more in the letter, but it isn't relevant. I read it through twice before passing it to my wife. She read it in turn. 'Hm',she said at the end.

'What do you think?' I asked. 'Is it true?'

'That,' she said, 'is something we'll never know.'

Notes and References

Prologue
1 *A King's Story* (HRH the Duke of Windsor) and *The Heart has its Reasons* (the Duchess of Windsor).

1 Background (October–November, 1936)
1 One of the Vanderbilt sisters.
2 As the law stood at that time, this would be six months after the granting of the *decree nisi*.
3 Prior to the Indian Independence Act of 1947, Kings of England were also Emperors of India – Empress in the case of Queen Victoria, the first to hold the title.

2 The House Party (November 20–23)
1 Partly destroyed by bombs during World War II, possibly in mistake for Windsor Castle.
2 Later 2nd Viscount Rothermere (d.1978)

6 Scotland Yard Investigates (November 26–28)
1 Canada, Australia, New Zealand, South Africa and Ireland.
2 Later 1st Viscount Monckton of Brenchley (d.1965).
3 Inspector Evans of Scotland Yard was the King's security officer.

7 The Journal (November 29–30)
1 World heavyweight boxing champion, 1935-7.

8 A Vital Lead (December 1–2)
1 Confirmation of this 'rumoured plot' is contained in the Duchess of Windsor's memoirs.

9   Flight to France (December 2–4)
1   Joseph Lyons was Prime Minister of Australia.
2   The King's Private Secretary.
3   Died 1978.

10   The Journal (December 3–4)
1   The Duchess of Windsor confirms this curious stop by the roadside in her memoirs. They stopped, it seems, to discuss a proposal by Lord Brownlow that she should hide out with him and his wife at their home in Lincolnshire instead of going to Cannes. In the event, she decided to stick to the original plan.
2   The memoirs of the late Duchess of Windsor reveal that her passage was booked in the name of 'Mrs Harris'.
3   According to the Duchess of Windsor's memoirs, it was 'the papers for the car' – not her passport – which caused the trouble.
4   The Duchess of Windsor's memoirs confirm the incident. According to her, Inspector Evans thought there might be a pistol hidden in the camera.

11   Words of Warning (December 4)
1   The diary of the Duke of York (later King George VI) confirms the substance of this brief telephone call.

13   The King's Decision (December 4)
1   The Duchess of Windsor, though she recalls her unsuccessful attempt to telephone the King from Orleans in her memoirs, makes no mention of this call from Blois.

14   The Journal (December 4–5)
1   The Duchess of Windsor's memoirs confirm that this was indeed the plan.

15   Royal Pursuit (December 5)
1   The King's personal pilot. Later Air Vice-Marshal Sir Edward Fielden.

16   The Journal (December 5)
1   The Duchess of Windsor reveals in her memoirs that the

Buick was actually driven round to an alley at the rear of the restaurant and that she and Lord Brownlow scrambled out through a small window above the kitchen sink.

18   The Journal *(December 5–6)*
1   The Duchess of Windsor joked about the telephone incident in her memoirs, but made no mention of the King.

19   *Memory of Things Past (December 6–7)*
1   Queen Elizabeth II.

Acknowledgements
and Bibliography

Without permission to publish the contents of 'the Journal' this book could not have been written and it is a matter of regret that the author of that intriguing manuscript is no longer alive. Nevertheless I acknowledge my debt.

My thanks are also due to the handful of other people who have helped with information or confirmation. For obvious reasons they prefer to remain anonymous.

In addition to the memoirs of the Duke and Duchess of Windsor, I have consulted a number of other books in the search for confirmation or elucidation. The full list is as follows:

J. Bryan III & Charles J.V. Murphy, *The Windsor Story* (Granada Publishing, 1979)

(ed.) Roberts Rhodes Jones, *Chips: The Diaries of Sir Henry Channon* (Weidenfeld & Nicolson, 1967)

Frances Donaldson, *Edward VIII* (Weidenfeld & Nicolson, 1974)

Graham and Heather Fisher, *The Queen's Family* (W.H. Allen, 1982)

Robert Lacey, *Majesty* (Hutchinson, 1977)

James Pope Hennessy, *Queen Mary* (George Allen & Unwin, 1959)

Michael Thornton, *Royal Feud* (Michael Joseph, 1985)

Sir John Wheeler-Bennett, *King George VI* (Macmillan, 1958)

Duchess of Windsor, *The Heart Has Its Reasons* (Michael Joseph 1956)

HRH The Duke of Windsor, *A King's Story*, (Cassell 1960)

Also various editions of *Burke's Peerage, Debrett, Whitaker's Almanac, Who's Who,* the *A.A. Foreign Touring Guide*, and the files of *The Times*.

Index

(Place names in italics)